Excerpt:

I0826477

When James reappeared at the top of the stairway, Cathy thought her heart would stop. Dressed now in a blue blazer over a white shirt open at the neck, Dr. Barnett was a stunning vision. *The blazer accentuated the deep blue in his eyes. As he approached, he must have sensed the feelings churning inside her, "Are you alright Cathy?" "Yes, yes," she replied. "Great, let's head over to the Hacienda." He put out his hand and Cathy stood up, facing him, looking into his eyes. She could sense a growing mutual attraction with this intriguing man. When they reached the parking lot she wasn't at all surprised when he helped her into a vintage Jaguar roadster. "Nice car," she remarked. "It's an XK 140 drop head coupe," he said. It was a perfect evening for an open car, but as the wind buffeted her hair, Cathy thought "I'm going to look like a witch by the time we get to the restaurant."*

Dr. Barnett didn't seem to notice Cathy's hair as he helped her out of the Jag at the Hacienda Del Sol. The maitre d' greeted them, "Good evening Dr. Barnett, table for two? The restaurant had tables surrounding a large fountain in the central area and secluded booths on the periphery. A very romantic setting, Cathy thought. They were ushered to a booth by the maitre d'. "Thank you Manuel," Dr. Barnett said as he slipped a bill into Manuel's hand. "Enjoy your dinner," Manuel said with a knowing look and a sound of assurance in his voice as they settled into the booth.

"They make a dynamite Margarita, it is hand mixed with fresh squeezed lemons and limes. Would you like one?" he asked. "How could I refuse," Cathy replied. When the waiter arrived, he ordered two Margaritas with salt, on the rocks, and a Chili con Queso appetizer. They brought the Chili con Queso in a miniature chafing dish surrounded by tortilla chips. The melted cheese and chili mixture was a perfect complement to the Margaritas. Cathy was feeling as soft as the Queso, her attraction to James Barnett was overwhelming her. She had never experienced an evening with the emotion she was feeling now. The conversation became personal, "Tell me Cathy," Dr. Barnett said, holding her left hand in his and stroking her naked ring finger, "Why is it that a woman as desirable as you is still unattached?" She resisted the temptation to say it was none of his business, "Well, Dr. Barnett," she began, "Please Cathy," he interrupted "It's James, remember?" "Yes, I remember," Cathy replied, she had held on to the formality of addressing him as Dr. Barnett to try and maintain her emotional distance. She could feel those barriers crumbling as he held her hand and waited for an answer.

Living, Loving

Incognito

A novel

By

James Wray

Published 2010

ISBN 978-0-9829136-0-4

LIVING, LOVING INCOGNITO

Chapter One:

The sirens' scream pierced the morning air as the ambulance sped through the busy streets on its way to University Hospital. The paramedic on board placed an urgent call.

"Trauma Center" was the terse reply.

"Ralph, is that you?"

"Yes it is."

"Listen, this is Mark, unit three, we are on our way with a Priority One Patient, a motorcycle accident victim. We have no response to stimulus - serious head injury; you have to call in Dr. Alswerp. We don't have time to lose with this patient."

"I hear you Mark, but that decision has to be made by Dr. Buloize, he's the E.R. chief today." "Ralph, please get Dr. Buloize to look at these vitals we're sending in and ask him to call Alswerp, O.K.?"

I'm afraid we're going to lose this one if we can't get Dr. Alswerp on his way, Mark thought.

He could sense his patient slipping away as each minute passed. The drip of the I.V. seemed to be as sand through an hour glass as the life of this man ebbed away. He had made this trip to the Trauma Center hundreds of times, but somehow this trip seemed more important than most – perhaps it was the age of his patient – very near his own, or the twisted Harley lying in the road. Mark had just made the last payment on his Harley. Why wasn't this guy wearing a helmet? Mark wondered what difference it might have made to the injuries to this man that he felt powerless to help.

"Hey Mark,"

"Go ahead Ralph,"

"Dr. Buloize has asked me to call Alswerp and ask him to come in."

"Great, thanks Ralph." Mark felt a sense of ease flowing over him; he knew if anyone could save this man, it was Dr. Alswerp. In the field of cranial surgery, Brent Alswerp was acknowledged the world over as one of the best. They pulled into the emergency entrance and the ER head nurse met them at the door. "We have been monitoring the vitals you were sending in," she said, "and we are waiting for Dr. Alswerp."

Just hours earlier, Chase Hartley had guided his Harley V-Rod into the parking lot at Rudy's, a small family restaurant in a converted fried chicken franchise building. Chase and his friends liked to meet at Rudy's for breakfast on the weekends to enjoy his famous Cappuccino machine omelets. The machine fluffed up the eggs to produce an omelet that was light and tasty. Chase often wondered why

Rudy's hadn't achieved the level of success that should come with such a deliciously unique product.

Since Rudy's opened at 7 AM, they could have a leisurely breakfast and still get an early start on the day's ride. Chase settled into the corner booth. His blond hair and boyish good looks belied his age. At 29 he was young for a retired ball player, drafted out of college by the San Francisco Rangers, he had found limited success as a utility infielder. When they released him last year, he decided to look for a business opportunity but hadn't yet settled on one. He had always wanted to have his own business and believed this would be the time to make the move.

Rudy came over to the booth, "Where's Samantha?" "She likes to ride her own bike, but she got stopped by a light," Chase answered, "she should be here in a minute." "Are you having your usual this morning?" Rudy wanted to know. "Yes, the rest of the gang should be here shortly, there will probably be about nine of us," Chase replied. Rudy looked at Chase with a sly grin, "I heard you made the big move and proposed to Samantha, did you set a date?" "No, no, I'm not ready for that yet," Chase answered, feeling somehow flustered by the question.

The rest of the group filtered in and the conversation turned to their destination for the day. "I thought we would ride over to Rockaway Beach off Cabrillo Highway," Chase suggested. "What do you think Sam?" "Sounds great," she said. The group agreed and after finishing their omelets, they mounted their bikes and headed down the road with Chase leading the way and the others riding two abreast behind him. Traffic was light as usual for an early Saturday morning, and the roar of nine Harleys filled the air as they rode by. As they made their way closer to the coast, they enjoyed the brisk California ocean breeze welcoming them. Samantha was riding directly behind Chase and saw him motion to take the exit ramp at Sharp Park. Just as he turned onto the ramp, Chase turned to look back to see if they were following. Sam saw the van ahead of him stop suddenly but Chase didn't see it.

"C H A S E !" She screamed, but her cries were drowned out by the sound of the crash. Just as Chase had turned around to see if the group was following him, the van made an abrupt stop and he crashed into it the moment he turned back. The sound of crumpling metal was deafening. Samantha brought her bike to a stop and rushed to where Chase had been thrown onto the pavement. "Oh my God, oh my god" she saw his head was bleeding and he lay motionless. "Chase, Chase, can you hear me?" There was no response as she fumbled for her cell phone. She could hardly make her fingers work as her brain tried to remember the emergency number.

"911 What is the nature of your emergency?" the operator said. "My boy friend just smashed his motorcycle into a van and he's bleeding and unconscious, please get an ambulance here, hurry" Samantha was frantic. "Where is the accident located?" the operator asked. "I don't know,

Chris, where in the Hell are we?" Samantha was hysterical. Chris took the phone from her hand and spoke to the operator. "We are on the Francisco exit ramp from the Cabrillo Highway in Sharp Park, when can you get an ambulance here?" "What is your name, sir?" "My name is Chris Reynolds; just get us an ambulance please." "I'm sorry sir, I will dispatch the ambulance and police at once, but I need more information from you." "Is the victim breathing? Is he moving?" What is the extent of his injuries? After what seemed like an endless list of questions, the operator said "I have relayed the information to the Emergency Vehicle and they should be arriving in a few minutes." Samantha sat on the ground next to Chase weeping and talking to him as his friends formed a loose circle around them to keep onlookers at bay. The Police arrived and blocked off the ramp to traffic.

Mark's ambulance had been dispatched from the Trauma Center at University Hospital. When they arrived on the scene, the police waved them through to the site of the crash. Before he saw the victim on the pavement, he could tell by the crumpled Harley and smashed back of the van that the injuries were going to be serious. He rushed over to the crowd surrounding the unconscious victim and knelt down to check his condition.

Damn, he thought. Pulse, respiration, lacerations, it all added up to a very critical situation for this victim. His odds of survival did not look good. A young woman was tugging on his arm, pleading with him to tell her some hopeful news. “I’m sorry, miss, all I can tell you is that we have to get him to the hospital as quickly as possible.”

Mark’s crew started an IV and loaded Chase into the ambulance as they gathered information on the injured man. “Can I ride with him in the ambulance?” the young woman wanted to know.

“We can’t allow that, sorry, we are taking him to the trauma center at University Hospital and you will be able to see him there.”

At University Hospital, Dr. Brent Alswerp's accomplishments were legendary. He had brought fame and funding to the Surgical Department but was somewhat of an enigma to the neuroscience community. After publishing promising research papers covering his experiments and clinical trials in neural cell brain transplants for patients with Alzheimer’s and Parkinson’s disease, he abruptly left the research to his associates. He said he wanted to concentrate his efforts on searching for the area in the brain which he described as the center of our “Sense of Self’. Colleagues criticized the secrecy of his methods. His assistants were precluded from discussing or writing about any of their findings. Students at the medical school described some of the experiments in which they participated as odd.

“There were like 15 of us,” one said, “and they placed electrodes all over our head and then asked us questions like, “Do I think I’m a good person? What was my favorite toy as a child? They put us in this MRI and asked a bunch more questions. I didn't see what the purpose of it was, but as long as we got paid, it was OK with me."

For Dr. Brent Alswerp, the research was far from frivolous. Using new imaging techniques known as single photon emission computerized tomography (SPECT), in conjunction with Magnetic Resonance Imaging (MRI), he was zeroing in on the precise location in the right frontal lobe area of the brain that defines "who we are".

Brent was thinking about this when a call came in on his cell phone.

"Don't answer it," Ann's voice was adamant. They were loading "Adagio" with provisions for a well deserved weekend sail to Catalina.

"Sorry, Hon, you know I have to."

Ann replied with a weak "I know." The disappointment in his wife's voice was so familiar it was hard for him to hear. Their plans were often interrupted by an emergency call. Ann had learned to accept it as part of being the wife of a brain surgeon, but it was never easy. They drove directly to the hospital and Brent left with Ann's usual parting words, "Love you, Brent," ringing in his ears.

He made his way through several motorcycles near the entrance to the ER. He was wondering if he would be in time to help this patient that Dr. Buloize had called about. He was met by his nurse as he walked into ER. "I'm glad they called you in Margaret, this sounds like a serious case." Margaret, as usual, was all business; "severe damage to the frontal lobe, heart rate 90, blood pressure 82 over 45, respiration rate 22, no known allergies or drugs. We are talking to an acquaintance that was with him at the accident, her name is Samantha Pierce she was on a bike just behind him. That explains the bikes outside, he thought. The group met for breakfast and headed for the beach. The patient was leading and just when he looked back to see if they were following him onto the exit ramp, the van ahead of him stopped. He crashed into it head first and was not wearing a helmet. Patients name is Chase Hartley, 29 years old, professional baseball player and unmarried. His friend says as far as she knows, he was not on any medication or using any drugs. We have not been able to locate any relatives at this time."

Dr. Alswerp checked on his patient. Initial impression did not look promising. There were facial lacerations, broken nose and cheek bone and trauma to the skull. Dr. Buloize was taking care of the lacerations and broken bones. Visual examination indicated pressure in the skull could be dangerously high. Dr. Alswerp decided to relieve the pressure before sending him for an MRI. With pressure on the brain at these levels, a delay of just minutes can be the difference between recovery and permanent damage. He inserted an intra-ventricular catheter to accurately measure the pressure in the brain and to drain the excess cerebral spinal fluid.

With his patient stabilized, he ordered the MRI's and prescribed the barbiturate pentobarbital to put the patient in an induced coma to prevent further damage while he determined the best course of action.

Dr. Alswerp entered the ER waiting room and was engulfed by friends of the patient. Samantha Pierce was waiting for him. She was very distraught. She wanted to know his condition.

"What is your relationship with the patient?" Dr. Alswerp asked.

We are engaged to be married," she said. "I have to know, Will he die? Will he be paralyzed? Will he be able to walk, talk, my God, how is he? I am going crazy not knowing how he is." Dr. Alswerp had faced these questions many times in the past, but it was always difficult to have to tell a loved one that you just don't have all the answers at that particular time.

"We have stabilized his condition with an induced coma. This will give his system a chance to mend while we do additional tests to determine the best course of action." He knew this was not the answer she sought, but it was the only one he could give her.

"We need to talk to his family, have you been able to reach them?" he asked.

“I’m afraid there is no family,” she said, “Chases’ parents died in a car crash when he was four. He was strapped into the back seat and survived but his parents were killed when their car rear ended a tractor trailer. He was raised by his grandmother who told me about the accident but she passed away earlier this year. I’m the only ‘family’ he has right now, please don’t let him die, we have so many plans for our future!”

“There is nothing more we can do right now,” Dr. Alswerp said, “I would suggest that you folks go home and get some rest.” Everyone left except Samantha and another friend of the victim. “Chris and I are going to stay,” she told Dr. Alswerp.

After studying the images from the MRI, there were some that startled him – he had never seen this type of brain damage and decided it was necessary to order enhanced MRI’s to verify what seemed to be indicated by the original tests. When he received the enhanced MRI’s, Dr. Alswerp confirmed what was indicated by the original tests, there was a partial separation in the frontal lobe area. He began to consider some possibilities that were exciting him. Dr. Alswerp knew that if the idea that was forming in his mind had any chance of success, it was going to take a procedure that had never before been attempted. He would need the best neurosurgeon in the world to operate. He decided to contact a former intern who had moved to the Chicago area after completing his residency. He was young, but had enjoyed great success with new procedures he had developed for intricate brain operations and had been hailed by many of his colleagues as the brightest star in the realm of neurosurgery. If anyone in the world would be capable of performing the operation Brent now had in mind, it would be he. Dr. Alswerp asked his assistant to contact Dr. James Barnett in Chicago.

Chapter Two:

It was early Sunday morning. Dr. James Barnett sat on the edge of the bed gazing out the window of his apartment on the 92nd floor of the John Hancock Center in Chicago. He could see his "R" Class Sloop resting on its mooring in Belmont Harbor. He had raised the floor level in the bedroom and living room by two steps to give him a better viewing angle through the windows which wrapped around the entire building. The windows were above the heating and air conditioning units and without the additional floor height you could see only sky from a seated position. He reasoned that if you were living over 1000 feet above the ground you might as well be able to enjoy the view. A side benefit to the additional floor height was that it gave him the distinction of living higher above ground than anyone else in the world. Even his fellow occupants of the 92nd floor could not make that claim.

There were advantages to being on the top residential level in a 100 story building. On a clear day he could see the skyline of Milwaukee. Window shades were unnecessary, save for the occasional helicopter passing by or the unpredictable window washers. He often wondered what vicarious sights they must see as they slid silently along the side of the building plying their trade. Sometimes he would look out of the window and see a squeegee wielding worker a few feet away peering back at him.

His corner apartment faced North and West which made it possible for him to view the interesting path of Chicago's North Lake Shore Drive as it snaked its way along the shore of Lake Michigan. At night he could see a panorama of flickering lights in the city below as they blinked in various shades of amber and green.

Cindy stirred behind him and put her arms around him, pressing her breasts against his back. "James, must you get up so early on a Sunday morning? She rubbed his chest and thighs with her hands as she moved her breasts against his shoulder blades. " Ummm," James said, "that feels good but I have to get going." "How about a quickie," Cindy said, as she moved her hands to his sensitive area. She felt his body respond to her touch. "No," James said, "I really do have to be going." He didn't want any of his energy to be sapped this morning. There was too much at stake.

He stood up as Cindy fell back onto the bed. James surveyed her supple tanned body with the three small bikini patches of white. The upper two outlined an area not much larger than her nipples while the lower one looked barely sufficient for its job. A natural blond, James thought, maybe I was too hasty in turning her down, but no, I really have to stay focused on today's race. He summoned his resolve and said "Last night was fantastic, Cindy, I had a great time. Why don't you get dressed and I'll drop you off at your place on my way to the yacht club."

When she got out of the car he said "I'll call you later and we'll see if we can hook up next weekend." James had met Cindy a few weeks prior at a party and was attracted by her long blond hair and trim shape. She was a fun person to be with but not someone with whom he was interested in developing a long term relationship.

His thoughts were centered on the days' major event, the final race for the season championship in the "R" class. His sloop, Gypsy, was tied for the lead with 'Ariel" and the winner of today's race would take home the trophy. There were nine boats in the fleet, but it usually came down to a battle between 'Ariel' and 'Gypsy'. He was looking forward to the day. Sailboat racing demanded complete concentration. There was no time to worry about anything else that was going on in his life when he was racing. After a race he found himself completely exhausted and relaxed.

He liked to arrive at the club before his crew so he could have some breakfast at the buffet and have time to check on the weather. As he stepped out of his car, he felt the wind blowing through his hair and buffeting his face. "Great," he thought, today's weather promised to be ideal for the type of course racing that the club sponsored. A steady 15 knot breeze was blowing in from the Northeast, exactly the kind of weather Gypsy loved. He took the oars from the locker and as he rowed the dinghy out to the mooring he felt the wind on his back as it kicked up wavelets in the harbor. Gypsy seemed as eager as he to get on with the sail. She was a beautiful example of wooden boat building craftsmanship. Built near the end of the era of wooden boats, she was 42' long with a 50' mast. With a narrow beam, she relied on 8000 pounds of lead in the keel six feet below the waterline to keep her upright. A very powerful sailing machine, she required a crew of five; foredeck man, port and starboard cockpit winch tenders, main sheet /tactician and skipper/helmsman. James was enthralled by the magnificence of Gypsy's design. She was the epitome of power and grace at the other end of the spectrum from the boats James had as a young boy. As a youth, he sailed home-made hand me downs on the Detroit River near his home. The boats were fickle and touchy and would capsize with the slightest error by the helmsman. He always sailed alone and frequently needed the help of a power boat to tow him and his capsized boat ashore. He attributed his light touch on the tiller to the years of sailing the slender center-boarders.

The "R" boats had no auxiliary power, relying only on the wind, but this posed no problem, especially this morning with the stiff breeze coming in from the Northeast. James rowed back to the dock and picked up Ted, his tactician, and Steve, the foredeck man. Steve was the crew 'Adonis', his blond hair flowing in the wind and his bare chest showing off his sculpted torso. He wore only sailing shorts regardless of the weather.

"Great day for Gypsy, skipper," Steve said as he rowed ashore to pick up Peter and Ben, the winch tenders. Ben, the antithesis of an Adonis said, "Hi beautiful," his nickname for Steve as he climbed into the dinghy. With the entire crew on board, James gave the command to raise the main and jib. Ben attached the dinghy to the mooring can and James gave the command to "back" the jib and cast off the mooring line. With the jib aback, Gypsy fell off to leeward, allowing the mainsail to fill. She gathered headway as James guided her through the boats in the harbor and into Lake Michigan. As they sailed out to the race course, Gypsy seemed as eager as the crew to join the battle.

"It looks like everybody is here," Steve said, "Ariel's just under us to leeward. As the five minute warning gun sounded, Ted, the tactician, said the committee boat end of the starting line would be favored.

When one end of the starting line is favored, all boats want to be there when the gun sounds. James had devised a method to bring Gypsy to the favored end of the line at the starting gun and now began to implement it. "Trim" he shouted, to bring Gypsy hard on the wind. The boat responded with her 13000 pounds of displacement. Ted read the compass," 355 degrees, skipper." OK, we have our heading. Stand by to come about.

The crew was ready, "helms alee," James shouted. He steered Gypsy back across the starting line on a reach. "Three minutes twenty seconds," Ted announced as they crossed the line "ease off" James commanded. "We'll jibe at one minute, thirty seconds."

“Watch out for Ariel,” Ted said, “she’s right off our bow.” “I’ve got her,” James said. “Stand by to jibe,” James looked at his watch. “Jibe, he shouted.” Gypsy swung around, her boom crossing over the cockpit and the jenny coming in to leeward. Ariel was bearing down on them. “Hold your course,” he shouted, he didn’t want them to file a protest claiming they had to fall off to keep from hitting him. Ariel sliced through the water only a few feet astern. James exchanged glances with his rival skipper in this supercharged moment, like gladiators with swords drawn, James thought. He hoped he wouldn’t be the one to fall on his sword when it was over.

They were approaching the committee boat. James was mentally computing the rate he was closing on the committee boat and the amount of time until the starting gun. He did not want to arrive at the line early or all their hard work would be for naught. Ariel was upwind, right where he wanted her. He had Yankee, an “R” boat designed by the great Nathanial Herreshoff to leeward. Gypsy was hard on the wind and headed for the committee boat. With Yankee underneath him, James couldn’t sail down the line to use up seconds if he was early. He would have to cross the line and return for a restart. He could still force Ariel to come about and fall in behind him to keep from ramming the committee boat even if he was early.

Ted counted down; “ten, nine, eight, seven, six, five, you’ll be all right skipper, four, three, two, one, GUN!”

Chapter Three:

A perfect start! Gypsy was charging through the waves like the thoroughbred she was. This was her kind of weather and she loved it. Her powerful hull was attacking each wave with eagerness. The strong Northeast wind had Gypsy heeled over with her rail in the water. The waves were breaking over the bow and sending spray back over the crew in the cockpit. Shouts of joy came from James and the crew as the spray hit their faces. They were holding on to the coaming and loving it as Gypsy knifed through the seas. The "R" boats were designed for exactly this kind of sailing and Gypsy was eating it up.

"Yankee had to tack away," Ted said, "she was getting our bad air. Ariel is eight boat lengths dead astern."

"Great," James was happy. "All we have to do is make sure we don't let them get out from under us." The first leg of the race was a beat into the wind. It usually separates the boats as each one seeks a favorable shift in the wind. With Ariel dead astern, Gypsy was in control and they stayed 'on top' of Ariel and rounded the first mark six boat lengths ahead.

"Stand by to jibe" James said. "Jibe Ho". He swung the boat around through the wind as Peter hauled in on the main sheet to bring the boom amidships while Steve and Ben rigged the Spinnaker pole and sheets. "Up with the chute,"

James shouted as the crew worked feverishly to bring the boat into trim.

This was the most nerve-racking part of the race for James. The hard charging beat to windward with the spray flying over the hull was exhilarating, but sailing downwind with the wind at your back was like being in another world. Everything quieted down, the boat, the wind and the waves all moving in the same direction created very little commotion. There was little for James to think about save the relentless pursuit of their competitor. Ariel was directly behind them and beginning to blanket their wind, she had clear air and was bearing down on them until her bow was only a few feet from Gypsy's stern.

Overtaking boats must keep clear so James knew they would be careful not to foul out. "They're heading up Skipper," Ted whispered. James saw Ariel's bow swing off to the side in an attempt to pass them. "Harden up," James said quietly, "Trim the chute." Gypsy headed up into the wind to keep Ariel from passing. "They're still coming Skipper," Ted said. "Bringing her up," James said as he steered Gypsy higher into the wind. The boats were now sailing side by side, only a few feet apart, the crews exchanging furtive glances as they concentrated on getting the last ounce of speed from their boat. Ariel's helmsman shouted "mast abeam" as he reached the point of being a-beam of Gypsy's mast. "Holding course" James shouted back. Gypsy could not keep forcing Ariel up after she reached "mast abeam" without drawing a protest. "We can lay the mark if we jibe now," Ted said. "Good idea Ted, that will put them behind us rounding the mark, stand by to jibe," James whispered, not wanting to let Ariel know what they were doing. "We'll douse the chute as we jibe." "Ready," Steve whispered. "Ready," Peter, Ben and Ted said. "Jibe Ho," James said as they sprang into action. The main came in; the chute came down and into the hatch. Peter raised the Jib as Ted and Ben trimmed.

"Great work," James said as Gypsy came alive for the long beat into the wind. Ariel was only two lengths behind and tacked immediately after rounding. "We've got to cover, Skipper." "Helms alee," James said as 'Gypsy came about to cover. Ariel tacked again, Gypsy covered. Ariel tacked, Gypsy covered. Ariel was losing the tacking duel and decided to stay on her current heading with Gypsy now about five boat lengths ahead as they approached the weather mark.

"Rig the pole Steve, and stand by to raise the chute as we round the mark. Steve was busy on the foredeck rigging the sheets and halyard for the chute. He held the Spinnaker pole over his head as it latched onto the mast. He reminded James of Atlas holding up the world. As Gypsy rounded the mark, James shouted, "Ease the main, hoist the chute." Steve had done his job and the chute went up without a hitch as Peter and Ben coordinated their hand over hand hauling on the spinnaker halyard. As the chute reached the masthead it burst open in all its colorful beauty. James often wondered why sailors stayed with all white sails for the mainsail and jib but when it came to Spinnakers, anything goes. It was a beautiful sight to look back at groups of vibrant colored chutes pulling downwind but James had to concentrate on staying ahead of Ariel on this long downwind leg, the most difficult of the race. Once again the advantage shifted from the leading boat to the one behind. With the wind astern, the boat behind could blanket the wind from the leading boat. They could also use a downwind tacking maneuver and require the leading boat once again to try and keep them at bay. Gypsy had increased her lead at the upwind mark to five lengths, but now Ariel was right on her transom again.

James felt the tension building and heard it in the voices of the crew. "They're heading up," Ted said, the boats were so close he had to whisper to keep from being overheard. "Heading up," James said, almost in a whisper. Steve was on the foredeck watching what was going on in the cockpit and tending to his spinnaker. Ariel tacked away, but James decided to let her go and headed directly for the leeward mark. They were getting close to the mark and James thought Ariel was making a bad error by tacking away. "She picked up a lift Skipper," Ted said. James looked over at Ariel, Ted was right she had benefitted from a wind shift and was on a lay line for the mark. "Damn," James thought, "why did I let her get out from under us?" "Sorry guys," James said to his crew. "We'll get her back," Ted said. Ariel crossed in front of Gypsy so close that she almost caught Gypsy's spinnaker in her rigging. As they reached the mark the crew was on high alert. Rounding this mark could make or break the race. Dousing the spinnaker and getting the jib pulling again was crucial to maintaining boat speed. If Steve let the chute get away from him it could end up in the water and become a giant sea anchor. Ariel rounded up at the mark, dropping her chute and trimming sails for the last beat into the wind. Steve did his job with precision and Gypsy rounded up onto the wind with very little commotion.

Gypsy was a boat length behind but slightly to windward of Ariel, thanks to the efficient crew work. "We can't tack away Skipper," Ted said, "that shift that Ariel picked up lifted us enough to lay the finish line on this tack." James checked the heading they were holding and saw that Ted was right. They could lay the finish line on their current heading. It came down to two powerful racing boats, side by side, in clean air, charging through the waves heading for the line. It came down to pure boat speed and winning became the sum of many small factors, not any one of which seemed that important, but collectively they spelled success. Ben started calling the trim for the jenny. They had to keep the boat "on the edge," which meant not letting it fall off the wind or getting too high so the jenny would start losing its power.

James looked across at Ariel. To James dismay she was almost a boat length ahead of them but Gypsy had clean air. Everyone on the boat was trying to wring out the last ounce of power. Ted fiddled with the main boom to adjust the shape of the sail and Peter worked the jenny sheet. No one made any unnecessary moves. James and his crew were transfixed with the emotion of the moment. James said under his breath, "come on girl, this is what you love, let's do it." He kept a constant check on their progress. They had picked up half a boat length with about a half mile to go. Ariel was underneath them but she also had clean air. James felt the strength of Gypsy pulling them inch by inch ahead of the competition. If they could gain about another quarter boat length, he thought, they would get into Ariel's air but she wasn't giving up. Ariel fought back with everything she had.

Gypsy would not be denied, not this day, not in these conditions. James barely touched the tiller. The boat was in a groove and didn't need his help. Almost imperceptibly Gypsy was gaining on her rival. James and his crew hardly moved as they kept a vigil on Ariel. He felt the emotion building to a crescendo. James looked over at Ariel; it looked like they had pulled even with her. He looked at the jib, looks good. He looked at the main, looks good. Gypsy was heeled over and her rail was buried. He watched the water rushing along the gunwale alongside the cockpit, occasionally hitting the winch and splashing into them. "This is what yacht racing is all about," James thought.

"We're getting her, skipper, Peter said. "You're a little high," Ben whispered to James. "A hundred yards to the line," Ted said, "Don't fall off or they'll protest." The emotion in the voices of the crew was evident. Everyone was feeling the tension. With a lead of perhaps a few feet anything that would disrupt the boat could cost them the race. Gypsy and her crew were as one. The two boats, like thoroughbreds charging neck and neck to the finish line, kept forging ahead, powering through the waves.

"Ready to cross the line, skipper," Ted said as the committee boat fired the canon. Two seconds later, the air horn for Ariel's second place finish. "Great race guys," James said. "Congratulations skipper," came back from the crew. They eased the sheets and headed for the harbor. "Well done girl," James said under his breath as he ran his hand affectionately along the cockpit coaming. The release of tension was almost orgasmic James thought. If he was a smoker, this would be the time to have a cigarette.

Everyone relaxed on the sail back, they broke out a six pack and pretzels. The feeling of relief after a race was always welcome but especially today. With the boat secure on the mooring, they carried the sails back to the sail locker and went topside to the club bar for a well deserved celebration. "Thunderheads for my crew," James said to Lenny, the bartender. They sat around one of the large round tables with the captains' chairs and reveled in their triumph. Life doesn't get any better than this, James thought.

Chapter Four:

The offices of Lindahl, Martin and Barnett reflected the success of this group of young Neurosurgeons. The immaculate glass entrance and the reception desk beyond inspired confidence in the eyes of visitors. The polished marble floors reflected an air of unquestioned competency. Dr. James Barnett strode into the office with an assurance that comes from achieving success where others had failed. "Good Morning Dr. Barnett," Janet greeted him, "the people from Surgical Tools, Inc. are here to demonstrate the prototype of your latest design for operating room equipment." "Great, thanks Janet, "I'll see them in a minute," Dr. Barnett replied. "Also, there was a message on our machine from Nancy, an assistant to a Dr. Alswerp, asking that you contact them." Janet said. "Dr. Alswerp, really, I haven't heard from him for ages, please see if you can get him on the phone," he said.

"I have Dr. Alswerp on the line Dr. Barnett," Janet said. "Hello Brent, it's nice to hear from you," James greeted his friend.

"Jimmy, so nice of you to call, I've been reading of your accomplishments in the journals, you're building an impressive reputation as the "Brain surgeons, brain surgeon," Dr. Alswerp said.

"Whoa, Brent, I'm a long way from there, but what's up, to what do I owe the honor of your call? James replied.

"I know this is short notice James, but we had a young fellow in a motorcycle accident over the weekend. They brought him in with serious cranial injuries. Looking at the MRI's, I think if this fellow has a chance to make it, it's going to require someone with your expertise to perform the operation. I'm sure you have a busy schedule, but I would really appreciate it if you could manage to get out here to help this patient." Brent was persuasive and James wondered how he could refuse this request from his mentor, a friend whom he had idolized for years.

"I'll check my calendar, but I think I can make it Brent."

"Fantastic, thanks James."

"Janet, would you bring in my calendar for the next two weeks please?" He looked over his appointments and did not see anything that could not be postponed or handled by Dr. Martin. "Great," he thought for how often does one get a request for help from someone of the stature of Dr. Brent Alswerp?

"Janet, please see if you can book me on a morning flight to San Francisco," James said as he went to talk to Dr. Martin regarding filling in for him. When he returned Janet told him she had found a flight for him. "I have you on a United flight that leaves O'Hare at 6:40 in the morning and arrives in San Francisco at 9:19 local time." "Thanks Janet, you're a gem, you should be able to reach me on my cell if anything comes up that you can't handle."

Dr. James Barnett watched the lights pass by in a stream of orange as he headed out to O'Hare Airport on the Kennedy Expressway in the early morning darkness. He thought of his days at the U.C.S.F. medical center where he was chosen to work under Dr. Alswerp, they were long days filled with difficult ground breaking operations. It had been a very demanding pace, but he had learned techniques that enabled him to help save patients who surely would have died without those procedures. He had come to regard Dr. Alswerp as not only a mentor but a close friend, and when time permitted, he would join Brent and his wife Ann for an afternoon sail on their 46' ketch. James had often wondered how Brent had been able to snag a beautiful and intelligent woman like Ann. Brent was a great person, but he didn't normally travel in the same circle as someone like Ann. She was a Wellesley grad and probably twenty years younger, but they appeared to be very much in love; and from what James could tell, they really enjoyed each others' company.

After arriving in San Francisco he called Dr. Alswerps's office while he was waiting for his luggage.

"Dr. Alswerps's office Nancy speaking." "Hi Nancy, Dr. Barnett here, is Brent available?" "Oh, Hi James, no, I'm sorry, Dr. Alswerp is lecturing this morning at the university."

James picked up his rental car and drove to the university. He quietly slipped into the back row of lecture hall "C" as Brent was delivering his lecture. He had spent many an hour in this hall as a med student and it had a very familiar feeling. Brent was in good form, holding his students attention with his quick wit and rapid fire questions that hit like a boxers left jab. The subject for the day's lecture, as written on the board, was "Who are we?" and when do we become "Who we are?"

"I see we have the renowned Dr. James Barnett in our group today," he said, "perhaps Dr. Barnett would like to express his thoughts on our topic for today." James hadn't expected this and it stirred the same feelings he had as a freshman when called upon in lecture hall. He somewhat haltingly responded. "Well, I think "Who we are" is a sum of the parts we assemble over the course of our lives by making choices as to which of our experiences we wish to incorporate into our sub-conscious and which we chose to discard. There are, of course, some experiences we wish to discard that still make it into our sub-conscious. These are the ones we try to subdue through layer upon layer of subsequent occurrences, unfortunately, no matter how much we try to drown these memories, they still become a part of our psyche and as a result become a part of "Who we are". The end result is a frame-work that is greater than the sum of the parts because each 'part' is amplified by its relationship to each of the other parts." "It is through this frame-work that we sub-consciously approach each new situation and filter it through our matrix of "Who we are."

"As to the question of 'Who are we', this is certainly more complicated in so far as we consciously react to stimuli based upon our psychological frame-work. Our conscious actions then really determine "Who are we". We are constantly presented with stimuli and it is how we perceive it and how we act upon it that is governed by the matrix of our mind. . The conscious choices we make therefore determine how we are judged by society." James concluded his remarks with, "perhaps the simplest way of presenting this concept is to understand that "Who we are", is how we see ourselves, and "Who are we" is the way others see us."

His comments must have been received favorably as they were met with a smattering of applause. "Are you finished?" "Yes sir," James stammered, as he was still somewhat intimidated by his former mentor. Brent carried on, "All right," he said, "who would like to tell me where "Who we are" resides in our brain." There were no candidates to answer this question, and James was as curious as his students to hear his response. This is a question that has caused speculation and controversy for years among the medical community. He was anxious to hear Brent's' theory on the subject.

"Let's start with what we know," Brent began as he put up a large image of the brain on the screen. "We know, for instance, that experiments on subjects using functional magnetic resonance imaging (FMRI) indicate that our memories are stored in the hippocampus and transferred to the neo-cortex during REM sleep. We also have experiments using single photon emission computerized tomography (SPECT), that have shown a strong correlation between spirituality and changes in the right frontal parietal lobe." As Brent talked, he would point out each of the areas discussed on the image behind him. "There is no question," he continued, "that these new developments in electronic imagery have given us the ability to delve into the inner workings of the brain that were unheard of prior to the last decade." "The secret of "Who we are" my good fellows, is right here. And with that Brent placed his pointer on the right frontal parietal lobe.

As his students left, James came down and helped him tidy up the lecture room before they left. "Tell me Brent, are you as sure as you sounded about the location of "who we are"?" "Absolutely Jimmy, it has taken years of testing and data analysis but I can state unequivocally that the right frontal parietal lobe is the secret of "who we are" Brent continued, "I'm so glad you could make it Jimmy, I have a unique and challenging case and I need your help. As I mentioned on the phone, I have a patient with severe brain trauma from a motorcycle accident. He is in an induced coma to prevent further damage until I can determine the complete extent of his injuries and form a plan of treatment. I have run all of the indicated tests and scans, but one scan has intrigued me and I would like you to take a look at it and tell me what you think." "Be glad to, my friend."

They met at Brent's office and he put up the scans on the monitors. "This is the one that is so interesting," he said, and pointed to a scan of the frontal parietal lobe of the cerebrum. "Look at this Jimmy, the major damage seems to be concentrated in this posterior parietal area of the frontal lobe, but the trauma appears to have caused a partial separation of this area from the remainder of the cerebrum." Brent was excited by what he saw, I don't mind telling you Jimmy, I have been doing extensive research on this specific area for the past year and have identified a barrier separation between the areas you are looking at, but I have never seen a partial physical separation until now. I have ordered some additional views of this area which we will want to study first thing in the morning."

Brent's nurse Margaret came to the office "Samantha is asking for more information on Chase's prognosis." James was picking up some vibes between Margaret and Brent. You don't suppose, James thought, no, not with a wife like Ann and what he knew of their relationship, but it made him wonder. "James, I want you to meet my scrub nurse, Margaret Brennan, she is my right hand in the operating room." James was taken by her unassuming nature. She had the air of one who wanted to be appreciated for her capability and not for her attractiveness. Her dark brown hair accentuated her olive complexion. She looked very trim, James thought, mid thirties probably and tallish, maybe 5'10" or so. James could see why Brent was pleased with this very competent appearing woman.

Brent asked Margaret to arrange for the additional MRI's he needed and went to see Chase's fiancée. He found Samantha pacing in the visitors lounge. When she saw him she put her hands to her face and said 'Oh, thank you for coming Dr. Alswerp. How is Chase doing? Is he conscious? Can I see him? Does he need an operation? When would that be and what are his chances for a full recovery?"

"I'm sorry I can't give you answers just now, Samantha, but you may see him now. I must warn you that he is in a coma and will not recognize you." She wasn't prepared for seeing all the equipment connected to Chase, the monitors, the ventilator, the IV's, the drain in his skull. "Steady," he said, as it appeared she was going to faint. "I'm all right," she said, "it's just, well, you didn't see him before, you don't know how he was so full of life – will he be himself again?"

"We are still doing diagnostic tests," he told her, "and until we have a chance to review all of the information we have, we won't be able to predict his outcome. I can tell you that we must keep him in a comatose state until we are able to determine that his condition indicates he could withstand an operation."

Dr. Alswerp returned to his office. "Jimmy lets head over to the house, Ann is expecting you for dinner and she has the guest room ready for you." "Thanks, Brent, but I don't want to impose," James said. "Nonsense, let's go," Brent responded, "We'll take both cars in case you want to go somewhere later."

Ann met them at the door, "Jimmy, how wonderful to see you, Brent said you would be coming to help him with a difficult procedure."

"Thanks Ann, you look marvelous, Brent must be treating you well," James said. "Yes, that's what it is," she said with a wry smile, "would you like a glass of Chardonnay, Jimmy?" "We are having baked Salmon for dinner, a special recipe that Brent loves."

"Thanks, I would like a glass," James replied. "You cut your hair Ann, it looks very attractive." "Thank you Jimmy, I just got tired of dealing with so much hair, it was almost down to my waist before I had it cut. I like my Pixie cut although it took a little while to get used to it.

"It looks great Ann," James said, "And how have you been getting along? Have you had time to do some sailing?"

"As a matter of fact," Ann replied, "Brent and I were loading provisions on "Adagio" when he got the call about the accident victim." "How about you Jimmy, have you been able to get out on your boat?"

"Ann, we have had a great year, "Gypsy" brought us another season championship and we also won the Lipton Cup Trophy Series. I think the secret is in the crew, this year everyone on the boat knows their job and how it relates to the overall success in the race. The crew has been incredible," James was being boastful, an uncharacteristic trait for him.

"Jimmy, that's fantastic, I'm so happy for you," Ann said kindly, ignoring his braggadocio.

"How about a game of chess after dinner, Jimmy, we used to have some good matches," Brent said.

"Sounds good, Brent, but I have to warn you, I haven't played in a while so I might be a little rusty."

"All the better," Brent replied.

Ann's Baked Salmon dinner was everything James expected, a delicious blend of spices in a soy based sauce. Afterward, James and Brent retired to the den with their brandies and sat down for a friendly game of chess. Both players used standard opening theory and Queens Gambit for their initial moves. Brent was moving his Bishop into position to place James King in check when his hand began to tremble and he dropped his Bishop. "Sorry, how clumsy of me," he said, and picked up the piece with his other hand and put it in place. James did not mention the incident, but he was very concerned for his friend. A brain surgeon or any surgeon for that matter could not operate if afflicted with tremors. James was surprised by Brent's apparent lack of concern over the incident and wondered how long he had been experiencing this problem. He speculated on whether this had something to do with Brent asking him to operate on his patient. His musings cost him dearly as he made his moves mechanically. "Check and Mate," Brent said, and sure enough, as James lost his concentration, he also lost the match.

“Well James, I guess you are a little rusty, you normally wouldn’t leave me an opening like that,” Brent was savoring his victory. “I’ll see you for breakfast in the morning Jimmy; sleep well, if there is anything you need, just let me know.”

Brent and James turned in for the night.

Chapter Five:

James and Brent left after breakfast the next morning and headed to Brent's office in separate cars. James had the scans mounted on the monitors when Brent arrived and he immediately started examining them. "Just as I suspected," he said. "Look at the clear definition between these lobes, the impact from the accident accentuates what I have been evaluating now for months. This area of the cerebrum could be separated and replaced with an undamaged section." He heard what Brent was saying, but he had no idea how it could possibly have any practical application since the idea of brain transplants was not a topic that could even be openly discussed by neuroscientists. "You are not serious," he said, hoping for agreement.

Brent removed the scans from the monitors and replaced them with ones he had brought with him. "Take a look at these and tell me what you think," he said.

James studied the diffusion-weighted MRIs carefully, there appeared to be unusually high signal intensity in the caudate nucleus. He mentioned this to Brent. "Exactly, he said, and what does that indicate to you?" He wasn't really sure how to respond, but he did recall from his neuropathology course at the Medical Center, an extremely rare disease that could produce these indications. "CJD?" He said, in the form of a question. "Correct," Brent said, obviously pleased that he had been able to study the scans and discern the clues they contained. "From what I recall, CJD is a disease that strikes only one person in over a million people each year." "You're right again, Jimmy, CJD is not only extremely rare but deadly. At this time there is no known treatment and expected median duration is four months from the onset of symptoms."

Poor soul, he thought, this patient of Brent's' had drawn a short straw indeed. "Is there anything at all you can do for this patient?" James asked. "Yes, as a matter of fact, that is where you come in." "I don't understand," James said. "You see Jimmy," Brent said, "I am the patient."

Oh God, he felt the blood drain from his head, he was stunned. It was incomprehensible. How could this be happening to a man that had so much yet to give to his fellow man? He thought of Bob Douglas, his good friend who was his roommate at Med School. He had gone into private family practice because he felt he could help the greatest number of people that way. He had built a large practice of adoring patients with his friendly and sincere manner. He would treat patients without regard to their ability to pay and yet he was taken away as he was just reaching the prime of his career by lymphoma. He was jolted back to the present when Brent said "James, are you all right?" "Yes," he said, "I was trying to comprehend what you told me. Are you sure about the diagnosis? Have you had other tests to confirm that it is, in fact, CJD?" "Unfortunately Jimmy, there is no question. When I wasn't feeling just right a few months ago, I had a battery of tests run to see if anything would show up. When I compared the MRIs to ones taken a year ago, I recognized the abnormally. An electroencephalogram shows the periodic sharp waves consistent with CJD. I'm afraid there is no question about the diagnosis. I saw you noticed last night when I dropped the Bishop. I have been experiencing these symptoms for a while now. It is only a matter of time, a very short time."

CJD is a devastating disease Jimmy, there is no cure and there is no known treatment that can even delay its progress. Mental impairment, involuntary muscle jerks, blindness and coma can all occur in a matter of weeks. I don't mind telling you Jimmy, this just scares the Hell out of me!" "I have already noticed some problems with my coordination," Brent added.

James was having trouble wrapping his head around this scene. Here was his mentor, the man he had looked up to since he entered Med School, a man respected, even revered, in the neuroscience community, telling him he had months, perhaps only weeks, to live. How could God take a man with so much yet to give? First it was Bob Douglas and now Brent. It was not only unfair in his opinion, but in a field where so few really stand out as shining stars, why would he choose Brent? He could think of several of his fellow physician's who would not be missed, but Brent? It just didn't seem fair. Then he remembered what Brent had said, "Brent, what did you mean when you said this is where I come in?"

"Jimmy, I'm not ready to leave this earth. I feel I have much more yet to give. I can't accept that the Lord has nothing more in store for me. I want to go on, and I think this is His way of making that possible. The accident victim they brought in last week is a sign."

"How do you mean, a sign?" James asked.

Brent continued, "As I told you yesterday at the university, I have been working for years on isolating the exact location of our "sense of self" and by applying statistical regression analysis to all of the data from the research I have done, I have succeeded in identifying an area the size of a key lime that holds all of the identity markers that define 'who we are'. When I made this discovery, I never dreamed that it might apply to my own life. I have always envisioned the research to produce a benefit to mankind by being able to transplant this part of the brain in persons in our society who have distinguished themselves in their field and whose physical bodies were wearing out. Jimmy, Brent continued, I can now prove that it is possible to perform a partial brain transplant"

"But where do you find the suitable recipient for such a transplant," James asked, "and how do you reconcile the moral and ethical considerations of operating on the brain of an otherwise healthy individual. It seems to me Brent, that for now, you only have half of a process. To make a transplant, you need not only a donor, but a recipient."

Brent seemed pensive, "I admit that suitable recipients for these transplants would be extremely difficult to find. Accident victims would seem to be the only likely source, and even so it would require finding an accident victim with the precise brain damage to the right frontal lobe. Such a person would have to be of the correct age with compatible clinical characteristics. The probability of this happening would be slim and none but here he is, Jimmy, placed right in our lap. This is an astounding development. It has to be a sign, for it is precisely the unlikely combination of circumstances I just described that our patient possesses. The test results I ordered for him prove that he is clinically compatible in every way, so you Dr. Barnett could be the first neurosurgeon to make a successful brain transplant."

"Hold on Brent, this is coming totally from out of left field. I can't believe you are really serious about this. You of all people know that nothing even close to what you are proposing has ever been done. I don't think it is fair for you to even ask me to be a part of this scheme." "It is incredulous."

"You may find this hard to believe Jimmy, but I believe we are all part of this play that has been scripted by a higher power. You, Chase Hartley and myself, all brought together at this time for this purpose."

"Are you sure it is a play and not a tragedy?" James asked.

"Have you told Ann about your condition and your plan for a transplant?" James asked. "I have not told her yet, Jimmy, I wanted to talk to you first before I told her. If you choose not to operate Jimmy, she is going to suffer through months of agonizing care while I disintegrate into mush." Brent continued, "If you decide to operate, it will be easier on her regardless of the outcome. If the operation is unsuccessful, I will be gone and she will have to cope with the loss, but it will be a finite end that she can gradually recover from. If the operation is a success, we are in uncharted territory and I don't want to put her through the confusion and uncertainties of dealing with a hybrid that is unrecognizable to her."

Brent went on, " We don't really know what personality problems we may encounter Jimmy, and I don't want to force her into a relationship which she would feel obligated to honor but may frighten her to death. There is also the problem of my life insurance. If she believed I was still alive, living in another's body, she would be conflicted in applying for payment and knowing her, she probably couldn't accept it. She is entitled to that money, Jimmy, regardless of the outcome of our operation."

"But Brent," James started to say.

"No, James," Brent interrupted, " for Ann's own good, it is imperative that she be unaware of what we are doing. I'm going back to the house as soon as we finish here and try to explain to her what is happening. Jimmy, telling Ann is going to be more difficult for me than when I determined that I did indeed have CJD."

"Jimmy, no one wants to die, I don't want to die, I want to live. Give me this chance to live and carry on my work."

"I couldn't do it Brent. It would be murder. I won't be the one to end your life. I don't even like to think about it.

"On the contrary, Jimmy, murder is what you will be doing if you do nothing. What you would be doing is making a first step toward a goal of mankind since time began."

And what would that be? James asked.

"Immortality," Brent replied, "one lifetime at a time."

Chapter Six:

Ann peered out the breakfast room window and saw Brent's car pulling in the driveway. He had only been gone a short time since he and Jimmy had left after breakfast. He must have forgotten something, she thought. As she watched him come through the door, she could tell there was something bothering him.

"What is it Brent?" she asked.

" We have to talk," his voice had a gravity to it she had never heard before. Her mind raced through the possibilities; was there bad trouble at the research lab? Was there a financial problem? Was he involved with another woman? She was in a state of panic as he sat down at the kitchen table next to her and took her hand in his.

"What is it Brent? Tell me," she said, but she really didn't mean it, because whatever it was he came back home to tell her, she was sure it was something she did not want to hear.

"I have contracted a very serious illness," he began, "How serious," she asked, oh God, why couldn't it have been another woman or trouble at the lab, she thought, anything but what he was telling me. "I'm afraid it is very, very, very serious," his voice quavered, belying the manner he was trying to maintain.

"Go on," she said, barely able to make the words come out of her mouth.

"It's called Creutzfeldt-Jakob disease, CJD for short. It is a degenerative brain disorder, very rare and very deadly. How ironic is that? I have devoted my life to brain research, and I contract the most destructive, debilitating brain disease known to man."

"Isn't there something we can do, some treatment? There must be a way to fight this Brent." Ann couldn't grasp the implications of what was happening. "How much time do we have?" she wanted to know. "From the onset of symptoms, maybe three to six months, and it is not pretty, failing memory, lack of coordination, dementia, blindness and finally coma."Brent told her.

"When I noticed a problem with my coordination a few months ago, I went in for a battery of tests. I had MRI's, computerized tomography and EEG's. When the results came in, they didn't look good, so I went in for a spinal tap to confirm the diagnosis. It's true Ann, I have CJD, and it's only a matter of time, a very short time."

"Oh my God, Brent, what are we going to do?" Ann could feel herself losing control as she went over to Brent and sat on his lap. She put her arms around him and began sobbing uncontrollably. "Please, God, let this be a horrible dream, she thought, let me wake up from this nightmare." "I just couldn't keep this bottled up inside me another day without you knowing. We must work on a plan," Brent said.

“A plan? A plan? Ann repeated, we’re going to work on a plan? What kind of a plan can we devise when you could be dead in three months?”

“What I meant to say was that we would work out how to set up our finances so you at least won’t have to wrestle with money problems and investments. Fortunately, our mortgage is paid so you won’t have any large expenses to deal with.”

“What are we going to do Brent, how can this be happening?” said Ann, still trying to control her sobs. They sat there, huddled together, saying nothing, gaining strength from each other. Finally, Brent broke the silence, “I asked Jimmy if he would operate.” “On you?” Ann said. “Yes,” he replied. “But I thought you said there was nothing that could be done,” she questioned. “That is pretty much true, but I have been researching the progression of CJD in the brain and I believe there is a chance to stop the progression of the disease by severing the neural cords it employs. I have to tell you, there is a very low probability for success, but I would rather take this chance while I still have my faculties than to wait until I burden you with a totally pathetic shell of myself.”

“I don’t know,” Ann was stricken by the speed by which this was all happening. “I don’t want to sacrifice even one minute of the time we might have left.”

“From what I have learned of the progression of this disease, there is very little time left for us. I have already noticed problems with my coordination and balance, the operation is a long shot, but it's the only shot we have." Brent felt Ann's arms tighten around him, her breaths quickening as she sobbed uncontrollably.

Ann felt like a zombie as she went through the mechanics of living the next few days. She felt as if she was being swept along in a fast moving stream and she was powerless to stop it. She had nothing to grasp onto that could stop the hopelessness of her feelings.

Jimmy was still staying with them, but she hadn't been able to ask him privately about the operation Brent wanted. She finally had her chance that evening when Brent decided to go back to the Lab to recheck some data.

"Jimmy, what do you think of this operation Brent wants?" she asked him. She could see that he was uneasy and reluctant to discuss it.

"Ann, I'm afraid we are in uncharted territory here. Brent has shared his research with me and we have investigated several scenarios in attacking this killer disease. The certainty here is the increasing appearance of debilitating symptoms in a matter of weeks, followed by certain death. I wish I could give you hope, but I don't want to mislead you. The operation has never been done and truthfully has little chance of success, but Brent wants to take that chance and I think I would feel the same if I were in his shoes." Ann was stunned. She had hoped to hear something more encouraging. She could feel the force of the rapids swirling around her once again, sweeping her toward oblivion.

Brent had shown her where he kept all their financial records and made sure she knew how to track their brokerage accounts. She didn't want to talk about it, but he insisted she be fully informed on how to carry on without him.

At night, as she lay in bed with his arms encircling her, she wanted him to make love to her, but her desire was crushed by the impending doom hanging over them. She felt his arms stiffen and he began to shake and bounce around in bed. "Brent! Are you alright?" "What's the matter?" O God, he's having a seizure, she grabbed her 'phone and dialed 911. "What is the nature of your emergency?" She stammered through all the questions from the operator and felt like saying "Just send the damn ambulance." She ran to Jimmy's room and wakened him. He helped protect Brent so he didn't hurt himself until the ambulance came. Jimmy drove her to the hospital. "I'm sure he will be fine by the time we get there," he said. "Is this the first one he's had?" "Yes, as far as I know," she answered, and wondered, is this the beginning of the end?

As predicted, Brent was smiling and seemed perfectly fine when they saw him in the ER. "I'm sorry," he said, "I guess I caused quite a stir." Ann put her arm around him, "Thank goodness you're all right now."

He checked himself out of ER and climbed into Jimmy's car with Ann for the ride home. "Well, I guess you know what this means, Jimmy, we have to get on with it." "Yeah, right," Jimmy said with a definite lack of enthusiasm.

"Good morning, Dr. Alswerp, good morning, Dr. Barnett," Margaret said in her usual cheerful manner as they arrived at Brent's office the next morning. Margaret has been Brent's scrub nurse for the past six years. "I'm sure you heard about the commotion last night," Brent said. "Yes, I did, how are you this morning, Dr. Alswerp?" "I'm fine Margaret, relatively speaking, will you excuse us Dr. Barnett?" James waited outside while Brent talked to Margaret. He could see through the glass walls as Brent was having a serious talk with Margaret. Brent had to reach out and help her into a chair. He could see that Brent had his hand on Margaret's shoulder as she was shaking with emotion. James was sure that Brent had told Margaret the details of his condition. Sometime later, Brent and Margaret came out of the office. Margaret's eyes were red but she was composed. "Margaret has agreed to be your scrub nurse for the operation, Dr. Barnett," Brent said, "should you agree to operate you will find her to be the best you've ever had." "I'll do everything I can to help you Dr. Barnett," Margaret said. "Thank you, Margaret," James answered.

Brent and Jimmy went into Brent's office to formulate the plan. They studied Brent's MRI's and those of Chase Hartley's. "After you have the scalp pulled back and my skull opened up," Brent began, "You will need to follow the trajectory of the computer aided image navigation system to cut through the sylvian fissure and separate the parietal lobe from the central gyrus." "All of my research indicates this can be done without permanent damage to the surrounding tissue." "You must then place the parietal lobe in the experimental AFP solution I was able to obtain from a research project in London. This will enable you to maintain the temperature below freezing with no danger of antibodies forming when warming." "I must impress upon you the need to protect our data from falling into the hands of unscrupulous surgeons. It is easy to imagine healthy young men being abducted and sedated as recipients for transplants from wealthy individuals. Jimmy, everything about this operation must be kept in utmost secrecy."

"I don't think I can go through with this Brent, it's totally uncharted territory. The risk is too great." James said.

"Jimmy, this is the culmination on my life's work. I don't know where this might lead us, and with my condition deteriorating, we don't have much time. I have specified cremation if I don't survive the operation, which of course I won't. I have signed the authorization forms and I had Ann sign them as well. A few days after my operation when you use my parietal lobe to replace the damaged lobe of Mr. Hartley's, you will have saved two lives. Please Jimmy, as a doctor and a friend, give us both this chance for life." Brent pleaded.

"Look Brent, even if I did agree to operate, the OR personnel would report me to the state board and I would lose my license or go to jail or both. "I have that covered," Brent said, "My good friend; Andy Nerneau has been my anesthesiologist for nine years." "When I explained my situation to him and told him what we were trying to do, he agreed to our plan." "Andy is not like us James, if you know what I mean. I think he has a crush on me. If he wasn't so good at his job, I would have replaced him years ago because it can get a little uncomfortable at times."

"I guess I understand what you are telling me," James said. Brent continued, "With Andy and Margaret helping you, I'm sure you will be alright. I have sworn them to secrecy because no one must know what we are doing. You can imagine the media frenzy if this ever became known, it would set our research back for years. I'm afraid you will have to operate without an assistant surgeon because there is no one else I can trust."

James thought about what Brent had just said. We are planning a delicate, pioneering operation that has never been attempted and he would have to do it without his assistant. He was impressed with Brent's ability to ensnare Margaret and Dr. Nerneau in his scheme. At least he would have company in his jail cell. James was well aware that the first step in Brent's plan involved a form of assisted suicide, which was illegal in California. In fact, he was sure assisted suicide was illegal anywhere when performed with a scalpel. James thought about Brent's' chances without the operation. His condition would rapidly deteriorate, tremors and seizures would become more and more severe and he would lose control of bodily functions, likely in a matter of weeks. He didn't like the thought of Ann having to cope with this burden. Chase Hartley, on the other hand, would probably just remain in a comatose state for the rest of his life. James had always been a "Damn the torpedoes, full speed ahead!" type of person and he figured this probably wasn't the time to change. He weighed the pros and cons of performing the operation and decided to go ahead.

Chapter Seven:

It was 6:30AM when Dr. Barnett arrived in the pre-opt area to see Brent. "Good morning Brent, good morning Ann," he said, knowing it was anything but a good morning. "Good morning Jimmy," Brent said. Ann ran her hand over Brent's barren scalp, "Doesn't he look cute with his shaved head?" Ann said, in an attempt for levity. "Best looking cue ball I've seen," James replied, I'll see you in the OR Brent." Ann followed James out. She grabbed his hands in hers and looked up into his eyes. "He's everything I have, Jimmy," she said in a manner that was not waiting for an answer. "I'll do my best," James replied. He wished Ann could have known the whole plan, but Brent had been adamant in declaring absolute secrecy was necessary.

Brent was brought into the operating room and James began the protocol. I am Dr. Barnett. Our patient is Dr. Brent Alswerp as identified by his wrist band and medical chart. Would you state your name Dr.? "Brent Alswerp." "What surgery are you expecting this morning?" "Complete craniectomy," Brent answered, thinking of the hundreds of times he had been on the other side of the questions and he was sure no one had ever heard a patient reply "complete craniectomy." James continued, paying no attention to Brent's response. "Equipment we will utilize this morning consists of computer aided image navigation and inter-operative MRI. The protocol seemed a little silly this morning considering the circumstances.

"Dr. Andrew Nerneau, board certified anesthesiologist, I will be administering propofol and remifentanil while monitoring blood pressure, pulse, respiration and temperature."

"Margaret Brennan, RN, Scrub nurse, I will assist the surgeons by supplying and maintaining the proper instrumentation."

With the protocol completed, Dr. Alswerp was placed on the operating table and prepared for the surgery. James bent over and whispered in Brent's ear, "May God have mercy on us." "Go for it Jimmy," Brent whispered back. It would be the last words he would utter.

When Dr. Nerneau said Brent was properly sedated, James looked at the clock, it was 8:15, he took the scalpel and began to open up the scalp by following the line he had drawn earlier. He cut a large section of the skull and removed it. He cut through the sylvian fissure and began following the computer mapped trajectory he and Brent had worked out. He saw the concern in the eyes of Dr. Nerneau and Margaret. He had to forge ahead until he had the complete parietal lobe separated. Respiration stopped, pressure and pulse flat lined. We're losing him Dr. Barnett. "I need to finish," James said, and continued with the separation until he had the entire parietal lobe intact! "Vessel, Margaret," he placed the lobe into the freezing solution. He saw the concerned expression on Dr. Nerneau. Dr. Nerneau removed his mask and said "May God have mercy on us." Exactly, James thought, and then said aloud, "May God have mercy on us." Margaret was seemingly in shock, but managed her own, "May God have mercy on us." James looked at the clock, it was 12:45. The first phase of Brent's plan was complete. James made arrangements for Brent's body to be taken to the crematorium and met with Dr. Nerneau and Margaret to schedule phase two of Brent's plan. They all agreed it should be done the next day. "We can't let that vessel out of our sight," James said, "It must be stored at twenty nine degrees Fahrenheit." "I will take it home and keep it in my refrigerator, I can set it to the correct temperature," Margaret said. They packed the vessel with dry ice for its trip to Margaret's.

The security guard at the hospital entrance saw the container Margaret was carrying and said "Taking your work home with you tonight Margaret?" "You know what they say, a woman's work is never done," she answered, pleased that he did not want to look in the container. When she arrived home, she set her refrigerator at 29 degrees. She removed the vessel with Brent's frontal parietal lobe and placed it on the rack. She looked at the lobe floating in the solution, "That's all that's left of you, my beloved Dr. Alswerp." "You never knew how I loved you from afar all these years and how I would lie in bed at night and fantasize about you touching me and caressing me. Now I have you all to myself and all I can do is look at this little piece of you and wonder if you will ever again be my Dr. Alswerp." Margaret reluctantly closed the refrigerator door and decided to go to Luigi's for dinner. It was a small, intimate restaurant and Margaret felt comfortable there. Tonight she needed to be in familiar surroundings as her mind was whirling with the events of the day.

“Good evening, Ms. Brennan,” the maitre d’ said as he led her to her usual table. “Will you be having a glass of wine tonight?” he asked. “Yes, I’ll have a glass of Merlot and an order of Pollo Contadina for dinner.” She sipped her glass of Merlot and thought about what had happened the past few days. She was shocked and saddened when Dr. Alswerp told her about his disease. It didn’t seem fair to her that a man of his ability should be struck down by such a rare and destructive illness. She had loved the man from the first time she went to work for him. She knew it would never come to anything because he was devoted to his wife, Ann, but it didn’t keep her from wanting him every day she was with him. She thought about Dr. Barnett cutting into Dr. Alswerp’s head and removing his frontal lobe. She thought about the lobe residing in her refrigerator. If someone had told her a few days ago that all this would come to pass, she would have said preposterous!”

She finished her dinner and walked back to her apartment. The events of the day were weighing on her as she made her way slowly up the stairs and the burden seemed to grow with each step. She would be glad when tomorrow was over. That night she lay in bed and prayed the transplant would be a success and that all this would not be for naught.

James turned his thoughts to telling Ann the news. She was waiting in the lounge, as he approached he could see her trying to read his expression for clues to the answer she desperately wanted. She stood up and looked in his eyes. "I'm sorry," he said. Ann crumbled, but he caught her and helped her back to the chair. "I thought I was ready for the worst," she sobbed, "But I have never felt so alone, so abandoned." "Let me drive you home, Ann." James helped her to the car and they drove home in silence. "I was planning on moving into the apartment at the hospital tonight," he said as they approached the door. "Please stay tonight James, my mother is on her way and she should be here tomorrow and I think Brent's brother and his wife are also coming but I don't want to be alone tonight. "Of course I'll stay Ann," he wasn't really looking forward to being alone either.

"Would you like me to take you somewhere to have dinner Ann?" "Thanks, Jimmy, but I am not really hungry and I don't feel like going out, but you go ahead if you would like, or I can fix you a frozen dinner." Ann said. "Frozen dinner sounds great, but I can fix it." He looked in the freezer and found an Asian Shrimp dinner. "Perfect," he said and pitched it in the microwave.
After dinner he settled in for some serious TV watching. He didn't want to have to think about anything tonight.
"Where does Brent keep his liquor supply Ann?"

"I'm sorry, Jimmy, I should have offered you something, it's in this cabinet."

"A fine array indeed," James said and selected a bottle of Grand Marnier Cognac. "Excellent," he said and found a snifter and went back to the TV to pour a drink and relax. TV does serve a purpose sometimes, he thought, as a place to park your brain when you don't want to be disturbed by the thoughts that might creep in.

"I'm going to bed, Jimmy, I'll see you in the morning"

"Good night Ann" James wished he could offer her some comfort, but he couldn't find the words. He put his feet back up on the ottoman and went back to "The Tonight Show." He was starting a rerun of "Gunsmoke" when Ann returned.

"I can't sleep, do you mind if I watch a little TV with you?" she said.

"Of course not," he moved the pillow that was next to him on the couch and she sat down beside him. He instinctively put his arm around her. There was a bond of sorrow between them that seeped into their consciousness that was more reassuring by the closeness of their bodies. Neither spoke, the compassion they felt for each other was understood without the necessity of conversation. James felt the warmth and softness of her body through her night clothes as she began quietly weeping. He put his other arm around her and held her close as her body pulsated with long uncontrollable sobbing. She let out her grief as she held on tightly to James for support. Her sobbing gradually subsided and she began to relax. "I'm sorry Jimmy; I didn't want to make this more difficult for you." "Don't be silly Ann; you know I will always be here for you." They held on to each other, comforted by their common grief until Ann drifted off to sleep. James wondered what the future would hold for this intelligent and attractive woman. Her life had been shattered, but she would certainly find happiness again. James felt peace for the first time that day as he lapsed into sleep.

James left in the morning without waking Ann. He knew sleep was going to be a rare commodity for a while and wanted her to get as much rest as possible. He left a note on the kitchen counter telling her he would return later to pack for his move to the hospital apartment.

Chapter Eight:

When James arrived at Brent's office the next morning, Margaret was already there.

"We were able to schedule the OR for 11AM," she said, sounding somewhat agitated. "We have the authorization papers made out for his fiancée to sign when she arrives. We were able to determine that she has power of attorney for the patient." "You seem upset, Margaret, is anything wrong?" James asked. "I can't help thinking about Dr. Alswerp, she said, "This has happened so quickly; the way he chose to go, the transplant and all, I just don't know if we are doing the right thing."

"I know exactly how you feel," James replied, "I am having a hard time with this myself. Dr. Alswerp was a brilliant researcher, and he was convinced a parietal lobe transplant was feasible and if Mr. Hartley has any chance for a normal life, this is it. I think we have to finish the job Margaret, and hope this all works out."

James took the authorization papers and left to meet Samantha who had arrived at the surgical waiting room. "We will be performing a craniotomy on your fiancée this morning to repair his damaged brain tissue and I would appreciate your signing these papers to allow us to proceed," James said.

“Where is Dr. Alswerp?” Sam asked, “I heard he had an emergency operation and died on the operating table.”

“What you heard is, unfortunately, true,” James replied.

“What happens if I don’t sign?” Sam wanted to know.

“You will be condemning Mr. Hartley to a hospital bed for the rest of his life, this is his only chance for a life without constant care.”

“That doesn’t leave me much choice, does it? If I don’t sign, he’s a vegetable, if I do sign, he could live a normal life, or die on the operating table.” Sam didn’t like the options, but decided to sign the authorization.

James and Margaret and Dr. Nerneau were silent as they scrubbed up for the operation. They fully realized the gravity of their actions and they were trying to deal with the feeling of being caught up in something much bigger than they had anticipated and now seemed to be spiraling out of control.

Chase Hartley was wheeled into the operating room and the familiar protocol began.

“The patient is Mr. Chase Hartley, as identified by his wrist band and medical chart. A 29 year old male suffering from severe cerebral trauma,” Dr. Barnett began as he glanced at the clock, it was 11:15AM. “Equipment we will utilize this morning consists of computer aided image navigation and inter-operative MRI.”

"Dr. Andrew Nerneau, board certified anesthesiologist, I will be monitoring blood pressure, pulse, respiration and temperature."

"Margaret Brennan, RN, Scrub nurse, I will assist the surgeons by supplying and maintaining the proper instrumentation."

With the protocol completed, Chase Hartley was placed on the operating table and prepared for the operation. When Dr. Nerneau indicated James could begin, he took the scalpel and began to open up the scalp by following the line he had drawn earlier. "Here we go," he said more or less to himself, "Now comes the hard part." He cut a large section of the skull and removed it. He cut through the sylvian fissure and began following the computer mapped trajectory he had used for removing Brent's lobe. He continued until he had the complete parietal lobe separated. He looked at Dr. Nerneau, "vitals acceptable, respiration, pressure and pulse OK to proceed." "Thank you," James said, and continued with the separation until he had the entire parietal lobe removed! "Vessel, Margaret," he removed the lobe from the freezing solution. Now began the tedious task of attaching the neural connections from Brent's lobe to Chase's. He had never performed such a complicated and delicate surgery, he thought this could not be possible without computer assistance. At times it seemed like he was a spectator and the computer was taking over the surgery. He labored on, caught up in the drama and complexity of his task. Finally, it was done! The sylvian fissure was closed and the skull section was replaced and bandaged. "It's over," he announced to Margaret and Dr. Nerneau. A sense of relief gripped them and a spontaneous three way hug ensued. "Okay," Dr. Barnett said as the 'band of three' separated, somewhat self-consciously, "let's get this man to recovery." He looked at the clock it was 6:30PM. They had been operating for over seven hours.

He stayed with Chase in the recovery room until his condition stabilized and he left word to be called immediately if any of his patients' vitals changed. He stopped at the waiting room to tell Samantha that Chase had made it through the operation. "Thank God! When can I see him," she wanted to know. 'He will be transferred to ICU shortly, but it may be a while before you will be able to see him. His condition is very critical."

James drove to Ann's house to collect his things so he could stay at the hospital to be close to his patient.

When he arrived at the house, Ann opened the door, "Hi Jimmy, please come in and meet my mother and brother in law." The scene was quite a change from when he had left earlier. Ann had perked up, "mother, this is Dr. Barnett, he was an understudy of Brent's and we became good friends." "I'm pleased to meet you." He could have easily picked her out of a crowd as Ann's mother. Ann was a carbon copy, just 20 years younger. "I'm sorry about Brent," he said, "He was a giant in his field and an inspiration to me."

"I'm sure you did all you could, it is just so sudden. It seems like he was here one day and then gone without warning, but we'll get through this, Ann is a very strong girl." "Thanks, mom," Ann said, "Jimmy, come and meet Brent's brother and his wife." Ann led him into the great room. It seemed an eternity since he had left her that morning sleeping on the couch. That couch now had two other inhabitants.

"Jimmy, this is Henry, Brent's brother, and his wife Irma," Ann said.

"Nice to meet you both, I'm sorry about your brother," he said. "Yes, a tragedy," Henry said, "What exactly is the disease that killed him?" It's called Creutzfeldt-Jakob Disease or CJD," James replied. "It is a degenerative, invariably fatal brain disorder. Life expectancy averages four months from the time symptoms are noticed. There is no known cure."

"From what you say," Henry asked, "what was it that you hoped to accomplish with the operation?" James did not like the direction this conversation was taking. "Well," he began, "Brent, as you probably know, had an insatiable quest for knowledge and was one of this country's top neurological researchers. The irony of being struck down by this disease was not lost on him. He saw an opportunity to look for a way to fight a disease that strikes only one person out of a million, but had chosen him. He studied computer enhanced MRI images of his brain and concluded there might be a way to arrest the disease through an intricate operation. I didn't want to do the operation, but he pleaded with me and convinced me there was a possibility of success. I did my best, but we lost him on the table."

"I see," Henry said.

The way he said it, James could tell that he didn't really "see" at all. James gathered his clothes together and made his goodbyes to Ann and the others. He headed back to the hospital to stay at the small apartment that Brent had adjacent to his office. From here he would be able to keep close tabs on the progress of his patient.

"Samantha Pierce has been asking to see you," Margaret said as he entered the office, "She hasn't left the hospital since this morning." "I'll see her after I check on our patient," he said, "have you checked on him lately?" "Vitals still looked good when I was in ICU about a half hour ago," Margaret said.

James went to check on his patient. He looked at all the monitoring cables, IV tubes and oxygen lines leading from the bed and wondered to himself, 'who is it in there, is it Chase? Is it Brent? He prayed to God that whatever identity occupied that body, it would have full use of its faculties. He left ICU to talk to Samantha. "I can take you to see him," he told her, "but he is still in a coma and has multiple support systems connected so he looks like he did when you saw him before the operation." "I would still like to see him," she said. Dr. Barnett led her to the bedside of his patient. “When do you think he will wake up?” “I am going to begin withdrawing the Thiopental we have been administering, but it will be a few days before we expect him to gain consciousness. You should go home and rest, we will call you when he awakes.” He told her.

James maintained a vigil at Chase’s bedside as he withdrew the medication. All the vital signs were improving daily, but Chase was still comatose. He began to wonder if he would ever come out of it. Samantha talked to Chase every day when she visited, but he gave no sign that he could hear her. “Chase, honey, wake up and talk to me,” she would say, “I need you to come back to me.”

Chase had improved to the point where most of his support systems had been removed and James had moved him into a regular room at the hospital. There wasn’t much more he could do for him, and he began to think about returning to his practice in Chicago. When he was left alone in the room with Chase, he leaned over close to his ear and said, “Brent, Brent, for God’s sake, wake up!”

He saw Brent’s eyelids flutter and open, “Jimmy,” he said. James knees buckled, he almost sank to the floor. He grasped Chase’s hand and held onto the bed for support. Thank God, he sobbed. When he regained his composure, he asked “How do you feel?

“I think I feel fine Jimmy but where am I and why are you here?” “Was I in an accident?”

“Before I answer that lets check a few things, can you move your arms? Can you move your legs?” “I think so,” he said, he wiggled his toes and moved his arms. “Fantastic,” James said, “and could you state your name, please?” “Brent Alswerp.” Do you know what month this is and what year?” James asked.

“I think it would be January because the last thing I remember is watching the Rose Bowl game with Ann and some of our friends. The year would be 2008,” he replied. “Well you’ve got the year right,” James said, “but you’re three months off on the month.” “Oh my God James, what happened and why do my hands look so strange?” Brent held his hands up and examined them.

James put his face up close and looked him in the eyes and said “Do you recall learning that you had contracted CJD?” “Yes, I remember suspecting I might have it,” Brent said. “Your suspicions were correct Brent, your CJD diagnosis was confirmed and you asked me to perform a parietal lobe transplant with an accident victim that was brought in to the hospital with right frontal cranial damage. The patients name and now your name, sir, is Chase Hartley, former baseball player, engaged to be married to a very attractive young woman.”

Brent’s’ face deepened in thought; “You are telling me that you actually made a successful brain transplant using my frontal lobe?” “Yes Brent, it appears that way,” James answered. “Incredible, how did you do it?” Brent asked.

"Actually I followed a procedure that you worked out. Dr. Nerneau and Margaret assisted me with a big assist from the man upstairs. You insisted on absolute secrecy and no one knows of this including your wife Ann who believes you are dead, which of course you are in the eyes of the world," James said.

"Do you remember anything of the past three months?" "No, I don't think so, but my memory prior to that time seems to be intact, I can recall the research I was doing at that time."

"Thank God," James said, "Do you have any memories that seem foreign to you? If so they would be those of Chase Hartley, the man whose body you are occupying." "No, I don't think so Jimmy," Brent said. James was ecstatic. "I have a million questions." He couldn't wait to learn all he could about the mental acuity of his patient. He left the room and returned with a mirror. "OK Brent, this is what you look like now and held the mirror in front of his face. "Holy crap, that's me?" "I'm a good looking guy, and young," he said.

James felt the tension that had gripped him ever since Brent had told him about contracting CJD begin to dissipate. The difficult decision to operate and the two long and arduous operations with seemingly little chance of success had been hard for him to endure. Now Brent was alive in this young man's body with all of his faculties intact! The emotional relief was overwhelming him and tears began streaming down his face.

"What is it Jimmy?" Brent questioned his friend.

"I'm sorry Brent," James replied, "I can't tell you how relieved I am that this has worked out so well. When you asked me to perform not just one but two highly intricate operations that had never before been attempted, I only agreed because of our friendship and my admiration of your work. Over the past few weeks I have been questioning my sanity for agreeing to this procedure, but now I must admit you were correct. We performed a miracle here Brent, and I think we have to thank God for the outcome."

"Amen," Brent said.

"Listen, Brent, this is the last time I will call you by that name. Dr. Brent Alswerp is dead. You are living incognito in the body of Mr. Chase Hartley, who survived a serious motorcycle crash and now has amnesia. I am going to tell your fiancée, Samantha, that she may come in to see you now. She has been here every day since you were admitted." "Have you got all of that?" James wanted to know.

"I think so," Brent/Chase said. "It is very hard to grasp James, but you apparently performed a miracle in successfully transplanting my lobe into the brain of this fellow Chase Hartley. I am now inhabiting this person incognito." "You got it, my friend, get ready for your fiancée." James said as he left to find Samantha.

"Good news, Samantha, Chase is awake, but he can't remember the crash and is suffering from complete amnesia." He barely got the words out as she raced down the hall to his room. "Chase, sweetheart, thank God. I was beginning to wonder if you would ever wake up," she was crying as she hugged him gently, her face brushing his cheek.

Whoa, so this is my fiancée, Brent/Chase thought, I am in a relationship with a beautiful young woman and I have no idea how I should be reacting to her.

I wish it was Ann, I know she thinks I am dead, but I would really like to see her.

The future is going to be confusing, he mused.

Chapter Nine:

Today is the day! Samantha could feel the excitement welling up inside her. It had been almost two months since the accident and Chase seemed like a stranger to her. It should be better when we get home to the condo she thought, she and Chase had been so happy there just before the accident.

When Chase had asked her to move in with him, she was afraid that it might mean the end of their relationship. She had seen it happen to her friends and didn't want it to happen to her, but living together at the condo had brought them even closer together. Now, though, as she parked the car and made her way to the hospital reception area, she was uneasy.

Chase seemed so different since he had regained consciousness. After spending three weeks in an induced coma, Dr. Barnett had allowed Chase to 'wake up'. She was warned that he would probably have amnesia and not recognize her, but it was devastating to hold his hand and look into his eyes and not feel the connection they always had. She had to tell him who she was and what she was doing there. Life together is going to be strange for a while, she thought, and now it was here, the day she would take Chase home. She had brought some clothes from the condo for him to wear home since the clothes he was wearing at the time of the accident had to be cut off him.

The nurses had been amazed at how well Chase had progressed with his physical therapy. He was able to walk unassisted only a week after regaining consciousness. Now he was dressed and sitting on the bed waiting for his release. When the nurse brought the mandatory wheel chair to the room, she told them Dr. Barnett's' flight from Chicago had been delayed, but he would be there shortly. As Chase had improved, Dr. Barnett had begun commuting between San Francisco and Chicago to attend to his practice. Sam was so thankful they could locate a specialist as capable as Dr. Barnett to operate on Chase; she didn't think anyone else could have saved him. She could see Chase was becoming anxious, so she got up on the bed with him. She put her arm around him and held his hand.

Finally the doctor arrived and Chase brightened up. "Hey Doc", he said, "Today's the day, right?" Dr. Barnett smiled. I think he was as happy as Chase to see the progress he had made. "Yes, my friend," he said, "Today is the first day of the rest of your life." Chase stood up and embraced Dr. Barnett. "I will never be able to thank you enough. I will always be in your debt." The two men seemed to be genuinely fond of each other. "I have you scheduled for a follow up visit in two weeks, but if you have any problems, I am giving you my cell number. I will be in Chicago, but I will be in contact with the ER here if you need help." Dr. Barnett wheeled Chase out of the room to the elevator. Sam thought here is a doctor that really does care for his patient as a person. They entered the lobby and Sam left to bring the car to the entrance. Chase stood up and once more embraced Dr. Barnett. “Good luck, my friend,” Dr. Barnett said, and Chase climbed into the car.

Sam drove as if in a trance, seeing familiar things but they would appear and then dissolve as if they were part of a dream. They hardly talked as they made their way home. They passed the ‘B and B Stakeout’, one of their favorite restaurants, “Remember the last time we were there,” Sam said. “Uh, no” Chase mumbled. “Shit,” she thought, “why did I ask him that.” “I should have known he couldn’t remember. I will have to be more careful.” “I am engaged to a man who doesn’t really have any idea who in the hell I am”.

Sam pulled into the parking garage and they walked into the lobby of the condo. “Good afternoon, Mr. Hartley,” Richard, the door man said. “Afternoon,” Chase replied. Chase followed Sam to the elevators. They entered the elevator and she pressed the button for the 24th floor. She knew from looking at Chase that this was all new to him. He had no idea where his condo was, or even if he owned one. Sam walked briskly down the hallway to their door so he wouldn’t feel awkward waiting for her to show him which door was theirs. He had bought the condo two years earlier as a bachelors’ pad. It had one bedroom with private bath and one large room that served as living room, dining room and kitchen. It had ultra modern furniture but Sam had brought in some “homey’ accents when she moved in. Probably its’ greatest asset was the great view of the bay.

Chase was wandering around looking at everything as if he had never seen it before. Sam said "I went to the store yesterday and bought some food for dinner. I didn't think you would want to eat out, and I wanted to cook your favorite, baked salmon with wasabi sauce." Chase smiled as he went over and put his arm around Sam. "I really appreciate what you have done, but you will have to be patient with me because I don't remember any of this." "I know," she said, and gave him a hug. It felt so good to feel his body next to hers again.

Chase was glad to be under doctors' orders limiting physical activity and sex because he was very conflicted in his feelings toward Sam. She was an attractive, desirable woman but he was not who she thought he was and it would not be appropriate to have sex with her as a surrogate. He felt very awkward in dealing with her sensuality.

"This is excellent," he said, as he tasted the salmon, "I can see why it would be my favorite." After dinner they watched some TV and then Chase said "I think I'll turn in, I'm feeling a little tired. He didn't ask Sam to accompany him, but he didn't say she shouldn't. Sam felt really perplexed, she didn't want to force herself on him, but she would have liked to share the bed with him. She decided to sleep on the studio couch.

Sam was awakened by Chase's screaming; "Mommy, Daddy, no, no," "Chase, wake up, wake up." Sam shook him by the shoulders. "I had a terrible nightmare," Chase said, "I was in a car with my parents and I saw this truck stop in front of us and we smashed into it. Glass was flying everywhere and my mother and father were crushed. I tried to reach them but I was strapped in a seat in the back and they wouldn't let me see them."

"I'm afraid that was more than a nightmare Chase," Sam said, "Your parents were killed in an accident exactly as you described. It happened 25 years ago. I'm sorry you had that nightmare, but maybe this means your memory may come back some day."

It's ironic isn't it, that I had a very similar accident years later." Chase wondered if other memories would be working their way into his brain. He decided to open a beer and watch some TV before going back to bed.

Chase was happy to stay in the condo and just take things easy for the next few days, but Sam was getting restless. "Let's go to PJ's tonight," Samantha said, "We have been cooped up in this apartment for a week now." "PJ's?" Chase didn't recognize the name. "We used to eat there all the time, Chase, but you don't remember? Do you remember Tony's Club? You have a lot of friends there." "I'm sorry, I don't recall anything of either place." Chase replied.

PJ's was a 'no frills', down to earth sea food restaurant with a loyal clientele. "Hi Chase, So nice to see you again," the woman at the door was busy trying to keep the wait staff and the customers in sync, but she seemed genuinely pleased to see them. Henry, the owner, came over to their table and wanted to know why they hadn't been in for such a long time.

"I had an accident," Chase said. That seemed to satisfy him and Chase was glad he didn't have to elaborate.

"What do I usually order?" He asked Samantha. Just then the waitress came up and said "Two Margaritas on the rocks, with salt," as she placed the drinks on the table. "OK, so other than the Margaritas, what do I usually order?" "You like the Sashimi," Samantha said. "Then Sashimi it is," he said. He was finding it increasingly difficult to find topics to discuss with Samantha that were of interest to both of them. Not many years separated them in physical age, but their interests were worlds apart. He couldn't tell her that he had lived through the period in his life that she was in now, and that he really didn't have any interest in reliving it. He was a 56 year old neurosurgeon in the body of a 29 year old athlete, and he didn't want to waste the gift he had been given.

He could see why they liked PJ's, the place was down to earth, the staff was genuine, and the food was great. "I'm glad you suggested this, Samantha," he said. "Please call me 'Sam', she said, "You always used to call me that and the only people that call me Samantha are my parents." "OK," he said, "Sam it is." They left PJ's and walked back to the condo.

He checked the internet for information on Chase and found that he had been an outstanding second baseman at Penn State University and was drafted by the San Francisco Rangers. He had a good but not great, pro career and was released last year. Reading between the lines, it appeared he had an abundance of talent, but did not always apply himself with the diligence a pro career required. Fortunately, he had not squandered the substantial income he had received and still had sizeable investments according to the records he had found at the condo. He knew he had to talk to Sam and tell her how he felt about their future.

"I just got a call from Alecia, she said the whole gang is at Tony's and they heard you were out of the hospital and they want us to come and celebrate your homecoming." "Can we go Chase, Please?" Sam was so excited he didn't have the heart to disappoint her.

As they approached Tony's Club, cars were everywhere. "Where do we park Sam?" he asked. "Just pull into the lot, the valet will park it." Sam told him. Easier said than done, he thought, there was a line of cars waiting in the valet line ahead of them, but they were moving pretty well. When they got out of the car, they were swallowed up in a sea of humanity. Music was blaring out of the doorway, "Good Evening Mr. Hartley," the doorman said. Chase felt he should address him by name, or perhaps tip him but all he could manage was "Thank you". Inside it was dark and loud. They started making their way toward the dance floor with Sam leading him by the hand through the mass of humanity when an attractive brunette squeezed up to him and gave him a big hug and a kiss. “Chase, we missed you, it’s wonderful to see you again, “Hi Sam,” she said, “follow me, everyone is over here.” He pulled Sam over and motioned in his best sign language, “Who is she?” “It’s your old girl friend Alecia,” Sam responded. They reached the table where their friends were sitting and everyone stood up to welcome him. There was a lot of hugging and hand shaking, salutations and good wishes. He was thankful for the loud music because he didn’t have to worry about what he said; they couldn’t hear him and he couldn’t hear them. He just smiled and nodded his head as they spoke.

“Come on, Chase,” Sam was pulling him toward the dance floor. “You go ahead, I think I’ll just stay here and have a drink.” “OK,” Sam said, “Let’s go Chris.” She took Chris by the hand and led him out to the dance floor. Alecia grabbed his arm and pulled him into the seat next to her. He couldn’t hear what she was saying but from the way her body was brushing against his she apparently still had some strong feelings left over from their relationship.

What the band lacked in talent, they made up for in volume. There were only three of them, but with their electronic background equipment they sounded liked a complete band.

Sam was dancing with another girl and Chris. As he watched her move to the music he could imagine what had attracted Chase to her. She was fluid in her motions, swaying, swiveling, rising up and then down to where her buttocks were almost touching the floor. Her blouse was loose and as she twisted her torso, her breasts seemed determined to get free. This is one very sensuous woman, Chase thought.

"So Chase," Alecia said, "Do you want to go back to my place for a while, I think Sam will be out there 'til closing." "Thanks, Alecia, but I think I had better stay here until Sam gets ready to go home." "That could be a while," she said, and headed out on the floor to join the others.

Chase felt guilty about being such a stick in the mud. He wanted to try and join in with this crowd for Sam's sake. He tried to travel back in time, to when he was in college and he would go out with the gang and hang out at noisy bars like this one. He remembered getting half smashed and bringing the girls back to the frat house to make out. He remembered, but it wasn't something he relished now. He just couldn't bring himself to get into this scene.

"Last call, would you like another drink?" the waitress said. "No thanks, I'm fine," he said. The band finally served up their last number and everyone headed back to the tables. "I'm sorry you didn't feel like dancing, Chase, that was a ball." Sam was really pumped and he could see she had really enjoyed herself. He was glad he had agreed to come, she deserved a good time after her long ordeal in the hospital. "Wasn't it great to see everyone again," she said, "How did you and Alecia get along? I saw her trying to climb all over you." "She was all right, she was just glad to see me," he said. "Yeah, right," Sam replied.

He thought about telling Sam what a difficult evening it had been for him. The feeling he picked up from the table of their friends was one of insecurity glossed over by the desire to have a good time. He wanted to tell her that her friends were not his friends, that whatever relationships existed in the past, did not currently exist. He wanted to tell her that he would have preferred being almost anywhere else, doing almost anything else, than where they were, doing what they were doing.

He wanted to tell her, but he didn't.

Chapter Ten:

"You may go now," the technician said, "I will see that Dr. Barnett receives these MRI's."   Chase really wanted to study the images but he knew he would have to wait to see them until his meeting with James. It had been almost a month since he had seen James and he was anxious to discuss his progress with him.

It seemed surreal, sitting in the waiting room to see James, who was meeting him in the very same office that he, Brent, had used for so many years. He wondered if his personal items were still there or if Ann had collected them. This entire experience was hardest on Ann, he thought, for she had no way of knowing that he had not actually 'died', but was very much alive in the body of this former baseball player. He wished he could tell her, but there was no way he could return to his life as Dr. Brent Alswerp. In the eyes of the world he was Chase Hartley and his future now had to be that of Chase Hartley. His musings were interrupted by the nurse announcing that Dr. Barnett would see him now.

"Please have a seat, Mr. Hartley," James said. He was taken aback by the formal greeting, but immediately realized that hospital staff could be listening to their words. "I was wondering, Dr. Barnett, if we could take a walk outside the hospital." "Certainly, Mr. Hartley, we can do that right now." They walked through the large sliding glass doors and along the sidewalk leading up to the entrance until they were safely beyond the range of curious ears.

"James," he said, "I have so much on my mind, I don't know where to begin. I could very easily settle into the life of Chase Hartley. Samantha is an attractive, caring person who is intent on trying to reconstruct the relationship she and Chase had before the accident, but I strongly believe the gift of this new life should not and cannot be wasted. I had devoted my life to brain research and the culmination of that work has resulted in an astounding breakthrough in neurological surgery.

By performing the operation, you accomplished what the medical profession considered an impossible task. This was a historic milestone but one which we must continue to keep secret until the moral and ethical concerns of our colleagues can be addressed. It would be disastrous if our data fell into the wrong hands."

"I feel like I must continue to build on my past research because anything else would be turning my back on this divine intervention in my life."

"I completely understand how you feel, Chase, and I hope you don't mind my calling you that, because I can't very well address you any other way. I just don't know how you can fulfill this destiny in the shoes of a retired ball player."

"I am hoping you will sponsor me for my application to Med School, you see I obtained Chase's college transcripts and while they are not great, I think they are good enough to qualify me for admission. When I learned you had been appointed to the school's board, I hoped you would help me with my application."

"Of course I will, Chase, you know I am limited in what I can do for you in that regard but I will do everything within those limits to help you. Is this truly what you want to do?"

"It is definitely what I want to do, James. As a child I was intrigued by science fiction movies that showed brain transplants. I recognized the movies were fiction but it ignited a fire in me to learn everything I could about the human brain. I specialized in Neurology in Med School and was fortunate to have spent my residency at the Department of Neurology at the university."

"I never discussed my theories on brain transplants with my classmates or associates because they would have branded me a 'whacko'. You know this subject is taboo among Neurologists and I never could have convinced them it was possible to perform a successful brain transplant. But you did it James."

"Think about this for a minute, doesn't it seem peculiar or strange that we were presented with the perfect specimen for this procedure when Chase had his accident? He was a healthy young man with the precise blood chemistry needed for a transplant. His injury was to the specific cranial location required and he had no history of drug or alcohol abuse."

"Yes, I have thought about that, and don't forget," James said, "that the onset of your CJD reached a critical phase at that exact moment, leaving us no other options. I have not told this to anyone, but when I was performing the operation on you and on Chase, I had what could probably be described as an 'out of body' experience. It was like I was watching the movements of my hands, but I was not directing them. The entire sequence of events was being directed by someone else, some other power. I know it's hard to fathom, but I don't believe I would have been able to do it by myself, without that guidance."

"You know James," Chase began, "the probability of all these conditions coming together at precisely the right time is unimaginable. My research was barely concluded when I was struck with CJD and when time was running out for me, we were presented with the perfect subject. Then my good friend, perhaps the only surgeon in the world who could perform the operations, agrees to do it and is successful with both highly delicate procedures. You cannot deny it James; there is only one logical conclusion to all this evidence. *'God is on our side'.*"

"I have to admit your argument makes sense Chase, but why? Why would God be on our side when we are encroaching on His territory? After all, He is the creator of all life," James wondered out loud.

"What you say is true, but we are not creating life, we are extending it. I think He could have some very good reasons for wanting to show us the way. You see, in my case, I will now be able to continue my research into identity transfer. The future of our civilization could very well hinge on our ability to develop ways of affecting identity transfers on a large scale to lift us out of the quagmire that has begun to define our civilization. Think about it, James, if we can't somehow extend the lives of the great humanitarians in our midst, the turmoil and destruction on the road we are traveling could eventually destroy us."

Chase continued, "Each generation is able to build upon the technological accomplishments of their predecessors for continuous development, but in the area of humanities and the ability to live peacefully with others, we start at ground zero with each new generation."

"Wisdom cannot be acquired by reading what our forefathers have written, wisdom is acquired by living, and each new generation begins back at the beginning in their knowledge of interaction with other people and cultures. Being able to transplant the wisdom of great humanitarians from one generation to the next gives us the opportunity to make real progress toward a goal of peaceful existence among all cultures."

Chase was speaking with strong conviction. "By facilitating the extension of the lives of those who have something to contribute to society, we are able to build on the contribution they made and should continue to make for the betterment of all mankind. We have never had this opportunity before and I think it is a logical step forward in our development. It's HIS Grand Plan," Chase said, obviously sincere in his feelings.

"If your vision is accurate, Chase, you are at the forefront of a great evolution," James was fascinated by the possibilities for a new order in the turmoil of human endeavor.

"Then you understand why I feel it is imperative to continue with the research which has brought us so far?" Chase said. "Yes I do, and as I said, I will do whatever I can within the limits of my position, to help you," James responded. He looked at Chase, this young man speaking with the wisdom of an elder, and said, "Chase, you are old beyond your years." "Isn't that what this is all about, James?" Chase answered.

Changing the subject, Chase asked, "Have you seen Ann since the operation?"

"Well, yes, as you know I was staying at your place at the time and she was devastated when she learned that we were not able to save you. She had prepared herself for the outcome but it was still a shock for her. I stayed with her the first night after the operation to provide some support and we spent much of the night watching the TV to keep our minds from dwelling on your death. The next day her mother came to stay with her. Your brother, I mean Brent's brother, came with his wife and stayed for a while. It seems really strange to speak of you in the third person. I had never met Henry, and he seems like a nice enough fellow, but I wouldn't be surprised if we had trouble from him in the future."

"Why do you feel that way James?" Chase asked.

"Well, mainly because of the questions he was asking. He didn't seem to want to accept the answers I was giving him. I have enough experience with grieving relatives to know when they are only trying to understand what happened and when they have an ulterior motive. Anyway, I hope we don't have a problem with him."

James continued, "The last time I came to see you I stopped by to visit with Ann. She is still trying to cope and to adjust to life without you."

"I think it is the realization of what she has had to go through that worries me the most." Chase said, "I wish there was something I could do to make her life a little easier, before I 'left' I made sure our finances were in order so she wouldn't have to deal with that problem, but I don't know how to help her deal with the emotional issues."

"I'm afraid there is not much you can do at this point," James said.

They turned and headed back toward the hospital. Chase explained how he had wanted to look at the MRI's but hadn't been able to. James said he would have them released, but warned him that they looked absolutely normal in every aspect. "I hope you are safeguarding our transplant data James, if that information got in the wrong hands, it would be disastrous," Chase said.

"It's under lock and key Chase, I am the only one who has access to it," James replied. "I'm not going to schedule any more appointments for you since I consider your recovery is now complete." "But you know if anything comes up that you wish to discuss, I will be there for you."

They returned through the sliding glass doors and made their way back to the office. "Goodbye my friend," James said. "Goodbye James."

On his way back to the condo, Chase reflected on their meeting. He thought about James' feeling the hand of divine guidance as he performed the operations and how fortunate they were to be able to accomplish the seemingly impossible. It had to be attributed to a Higher Power. He believed that it was true. They really were striving for immortality, one lifetime at a time.

Chapter Eleven:

As he approached the condo, everything still seemed strange to him, the neighborhood, the building, the doorman, the apartment and Samantha! This was not his life, it was a good life but it was not his life. "Hi Sam," he said as he came in the door. She was standing by the kitchen counter chopping onions. Her long dark hair was lying on her bare shoulders and flowing down onto her breasts. She was wearing a strapless dress that reminded him of a sarong. He noticed that her slight build and amber skin probably came from an Asian heritage. Sensuality emanated from this woman, he thought.

"I bought some tortilla chips and I found some nice avocados, I thought I would make some guacamole so we could have Margaritas before dinner." "Great," he said, but he couldn't shake off the feeling that he didn't really belong there.

"What did Dr. Barnett have to say?" she asked. "I'm doing fine, everything looks good and I no longer have any restrictions on my activities." "Wow!" she exclaimed. He knew what she was thinking. Since he was released from the hospital he had been under orders, nothing strenuous, including sex. He had actually welcomed the limitations as he felt really awkward about the idea of having sex with a woman who Chase obviously had enjoyed many times in the past. Sam was an incredibly attractive young woman who had been shut out of his emotional life. It wasn't fair to her, but he had no notion of the kind of clues he should be giving her regarding their sex life.

"Hey Sam, I'm really tired," Chase said after dinner, "I'm going to hit the sack." If he could get in bed and fall asleep he could avoid having to deal with the sex issue.

"Ok," Sam said, "I'm going to stay up for a while and watch some TV." She was in a quandary, she wanted to get in bed with him as she had on so many nights in the past, but she didn't know how he would react. She watched the TV until she couldn't keep her eyes open any longer. She had been sleeping on the studio couch since Chase had come home from the hospital, but tonight she decided "to hell with it, I'm sleeping in our bed, the bed I had always shared with Chase."

Although this Chase seemed more like a stranger than her fiancée, she decided she had stayed out of 'their' bed long enough. She went through the bedroom to the master bath to get ready for bed. Chase was sleeping on his side of the bed. At least I'll have a place to sleep, she thought. She looked in the closet for something to wear to bed. She didn't believe in nightgowns and had always slept in the skin God gave her. She summoned up her nerve and crawled into bed the way she was born, naked! She carefully lifted up the covers on 'her' side of the bed and slipped in. She breathed a sigh of relief as she put her head on the pillow, she hadn't disturbed Chase. It was definitely weird to be lying in bed next to a man she knew so well and yet knew not at all. She felt a wave of satisfaction and comfort sweep over her as she began to drift into sleep. As if by force of habit, she put her arm around Chase as he slept on his stomach and pulled herself close to him. She felt whole for the first time in over three months. In her semi-conscious state it didn't bother her that this man she was lying with had no idea who she was, she needed the sense of attachment that she felt at that moment. Chase was sound asleep, but she heard him moan as she pulled her body close to his. She believed he felt the same exhilaration from the contact of their bodies as she was feeling. She couldn't stop herself. She pulled herself up onto him until her entire body was on top of his. She ran her arms along his arms and her legs on his legs. She pressed her breasts against the middle of his back. Her body was alive, every fiber of her being feeling the warmth and excitement of his body.

At first, Chase believed he was dreaming; he was experiencing the sensation of his entire body being pressed face down into the bed by the pressure of Samantha's body on his. He felt her arms on his arms, her soft breasts were pressing against his back, and her hips were moving against his thighs. He felt a churning sensation as he was pressed against the sheet. As Sam's soft, writhing body was moving across his back, her breasts would get caught on his side and then slide over onto his back and then off to the other side. He had never experienced anything like it in his life. He lay motionless, enjoying the ecstasy of the moment.

He felt guilty. He didn't know if he should be feeling unfaithful to Ann or to Samantha or to Chase, the person Samantha thought she was making love to. He knew he should pretend to remain asleep so Sam would get discouraged, it wasn't right to allow her to make love to a man who wasn't who she thought he was, but the sensation he was feeling clouded his judgment.

He decided he couldn't resolve the conflicting emotions that were bombarding him at that moment when he was feeling so fantastic. He would deal with it later, he thought.

He started turning over as Samantha slid off to his side. She rubbed her breasts against his side as her hands slid down between his thighs. She ran her hands from his knees up between his legs and onto his chest. She stroked him gently with her hands. He hadn't felt like this for years. He had to admit that Chase was better endowed than he had been. A young man's body and an old man's mind, he wondered what James would think about what he was feeling. He was jolted out of his musings by Samantha. "I want you Chase, it has been such a long time," she said, and crawled between his legs and began fondling him.

This was not the first time he had enjoyed this pleasure from a woman, but Samantha brought a whole new meaning to the experience. She slid him into her mouth until her lips were pressing against his groin. He had never known the intense, almost unbearable passion he felt as she buried him inside her. "You had best stop," he said. She sat up with a puzzled look and said, “You don’t like it?” “Oh yes,” he said “But I don’t want this to end so soon.”

She turned around so her face was at his waist with her legs straddling his head. She returned to what she did so well, and he put his hands on the inside of her thighs so his fingers were just touching her tender folds. She slipped his hardness into her mouth, and just when he thought she was as far as it could go, she would go further, and then further until he thought he couldn’t possibly stand the intense pleasure any longer. He said “I’m sorry, here it comes.”

He could feel the start of the most intense orgasm he had ever experienced. It began at the end of his feet and worked up to his buttocks, it felt like his entire insides were coming out with his ejaculation. His body started jerking with alternate clenching of the muscles and then relaxation. Samantha stayed on him as he erupted into her. She managed to keep him buried until he had no more to give. The spasms continued. He was exhausted. He could only lay there like a spent rocket. He wondered if he would ever get his toes uncurled. Samantha finally climbed off and sat on the bed next to him. “I’m really sorry, he said, I just couldn’t hold off until you were ready, I know this wasn’t that great for you.”

“Don’t feel bad,” she said, “If you could remember, you would know I can only reach orgasm one way.” “Really,” he said, “and how is that.” She went over to the dresser drawer and returned with a vibrator that looked like a giant penis with a smaller one on top making a large truncated "U". "You use that?" he said stupidly. "No, you do," she said. She saw the look of horror on his face and said, "You hold it for me." "Oh, ok, I can do that."

She handed the contraption to him and lay on her back on the bed. He had never seen one of these and he didn't exactly know how to use it, but it seemed pretty obvious where it should go. He slipped the largest part between her legs and switched on the vibrator. As he pushed it into her, the smaller vibrating part was attacking her clitoris. Aha, he thought, that's what the little one is for.

From the moment he inserted it into her and it started vibrating, she entered another world. Her eyes closed, her hands grasped the bed sheet and her breasts started heaving with heavy breathing. "Yes," she said and clenched her teeth. She began groaning and crying as the vibration inside her and the relentless excitation of her clitoris by the small wiggler was driving her into frenzy. She let loose of the bed sheet and grasped the back of the vibrator with both hands; wrapping her fingers around his and pushing it deeper into her. Her breaths were coming quickly as she lifted up off the bed, pushing it into her. She was jerking up and down rapidly now as she began to climax. "Yes," she said each time her hips were thrust into the air. "Yes, Yes, Yes," She screamed as she reached orgasm. She twisted her body like a corkscrew as she rolled on the bed, clutching the machine in both hands, pushing it into her as she enjoyed the last vestige of her experience.

He stood by the side of the bed, marveling at this incredibly attractive woman and the unusual way she had of obtaining an orgasm. He couldn't help but wonder what life experiences had led her to resort to this method of satisfaction. He watched her lying on the bed relaxing after her orgasm. She was obviously fulfilled, a faint smile on her face as she lay. He admired her young body, her firm breasts, tiny waist and smooth skin. She was in her mid twenties, he guessed, with so much life ahead of her.

"I was wondering, what do we do for protection?" "What a silly question," she said. "But wait, you don't remember do you? You had a vasectomy last year. We don't have anything to worry about."

Chase got back in bed and laid on his left side, he always went to sleep in that position. Samantha put her arm around his chest and held her body against him. He was physically spent and content but his mind was wrestling with the ramifications of his actions as he drifted off to sleep.

Chase woke up the next morning still feeling conflicted. He had let Sam make love to him even though he knew he shouldn't and what's more he enjoyed it. He wondered how he was going to resolve his problems with Sam as he sat with his coffee. Sam got up and came to the table. "Good morning, sweetheart," she said as she came alongside and gave him a hug. Chase said to himself, "Damn,

I wish I didn't have to bring up this subject now," but he knew there was no way to postpone it.

"We have to talk," he said. "I know", she answered, her face growing pale and pensive.

"I'm afraid we will have to put our plans on hold for awhile until I have time to adjust to this new life I've been given."

"Don't say anymore, Chase, I know you need time, just please give me a chance to show you what our life can be together."

"I spoke with Dr. Barnett about what I wanted to do with my life," Chase continued. "Now that I have been given a second chance, I told him I felt that I should try to give back something to the medical community for giving me this opportunity. I told him I wanted to apply to Med School and he said he would help me if I was serious about wanting to be involved in the medical profession."

Sam was taken aback. "Doesn't that take like ten years by the time you are able to practice as a doctor?" she said. "Not quite, but it is a long slug," he replied, "Med School is like four years and then there is usually three years of residency before you can become state certified." "There are also exams along the way that you must pass to move on to the next level." "Fortunately I was a science major at Penn so I have most of the requisites required to get into Med School."

“I can see you feel fervently about this and I can understand how you feel, but what does this mean for us?” “Does this put off our wedding for a while or does it put it off forever? What does this mean for us, Chase, tell me, I just don’t know where I stand, I love you and I want us to have a life together but you have to feel the same way or it would never work. Tell me Chase.”

“I’m sorry, Sam, I wish I could give you a straight answer, but I just don’t know. If I am accepted into Med School, it would mean living on campus and long hours of studying and if I graduated and was accepted into a residency program, it would mean living at the hospital and working up to 80 hours a week. This would leave little or no time for any kind of an outside life. If I am not accepted into Med School, then it’s a whole different ball game. I think if you are willing to hang in for the time being, we will just have to wait and see what happens.”

Sam was clearly worried. She sank into the chair with her head in her hands and pulled her feet up until she was in a fetal position. “I just don’t know what to do, Chase, It has been such a roller coaster ride since the accident, at first I worried you wouldn’t make it, and then when you did, I was ecstatic. But then when you had no memory of us, I began to worry all over again. I don’t know what to think.”

Chase was watching the mail every day for a response to his application. He had sent in his transcripts weeks ago and was still waiting for a reply. Finally, a letter from the school, it was asking him to take the MCAT, a pre-admission exam. At least it wasn't a rejection. He was confident he would have no problem with the exam and arranged to take it that week.

As he expected, he took the exam and felt that he aced it. He now had to wait for their decision. With each hurdle passed, Sam became more concerned, she could feel the life she had envisioned slipping away as each day passed. Chase wondered himself if he was doing the right thing.

Then it came, the notice they had been awaiting. Chase was accepted for Med School. In little more than a month he would be leaving to live on campus. "This is the day I have been dreading," Sam said, "I don't know what to do."

"I will be keeping the condo, so you will be able to stay here." He said, "I will take care of the utilities and maintenance, so all you should have to pay for would be your groceries. Your hairdresser's job should keep you pretty well off."

"I suppose so," Sam replied, but her intuition was telling her that her life was heading off in a new direction and she was powerless to stop it.

Chase looked at the caller ID on his cell phone, "Dr. Barnett, how nice of you to call,"

"I wanted to call and congratulate you on your MCAT"

"Thank you, Dr. Barnett"

“Please call me James, not Jimmy, but James,

“Yes, right,”

“Anyway, this is what I called to tell you, Chase, you had the highest score on the MCAT that has ever been recorded by the school.”

“Wow, that’s great news, I felt I had done really well on it, but highest score ever, fantastic!”

“You know, Chase, the school offers the opportunity to “test out” on many of their courses and you should take advantage of that.”

“Thanks, James, I will certainly look into that.”

Chase arranged for his dorm room and purchased the books for his first year at Med School.

“I guess this is it, Sam, time for me to leave,” he said.

“Can’t you live here and commute to school?” Sam wanted to know.

“I need to concentrate on my studies,” Sam, “I can’t do that if I’m living here and driving back and forth for an hour every day, do you understand Sam?”

“I guess so,” she said, “but I will miss you terribly.”

Chase threw himself into his class work and tested out of almost every subject that offered him that option. He was anxious to finish the requirements so he could get started on his research. He was excited about an idea that had come to him regarding identity transfer and he was eager to pursue it. If his research proved credible, he envisioned a means of identifying thought wave frequencies and capturing them.

Chase finished his final exams for the term and decided to go home for the weekend. He hadn't been home since the term started and felt like it was time for a break. "Hey Sam, are you home?" he said as he entered the condo. She's not here, he thought, I guess I should have called her.

"Chase," Sam said as she came out of the bedroom, "What are you doing here?"

"I finished my finals and I thought I would come home for the weekend." Sam seemed uneasy as she stood by the bedroom door fidgeting. Chase began to get the picture. "You, ah, you have company?' he said. "Some of us came back here from Tony's last night after they closed, and Chris didn't want to take a chance on driving home, so I told him he could stay."

"I see," what he meant was that he saw a lot more than what she had told him. Chris appeared in the bedroom doorway, buttoning his shirt. "Hi Chase," he said sheepishly. "Hi Chris," Chase answered.

“Well, I guess I had better be going, thanks for letting me stay, Sam,” Chris said as he sidled past Chase and made his way to the door. “Sorry buddy,” he said as he went by.

“I’m really sorry about this Chase,” Sam said as she approached him somewhat tentatively. “I’m sorry too,” Chase said. “You know Sam, a relationship has to be based on trust, and I don’t see how I can trust you anymore.” “Please Chase, give me another chance, this is the first time this happened since you left,” she pleaded. “Do you really think that matters?” he replied.

“Our engagement is over,” Chase said, “you can keep the ring I gave you, but you will have to be out of the condo by the end of the month. I’m listing it for sale.” He turned and walked out the door.

“Well, as the saying goes, it ain’t over ‘til it’s over, but now it’s over,” he said to himself as he walked out of the condo and into the sunshine.

Chapter Twelve:

"Cathy, would you come in here a minute?" It was the familiar call from her boss, Peter Crist, Assistant Editor of the San Jose Times. Cathy got up from her desk and went into his office. "I'd like you to check this out," he said and handed her an item off the AP wire about a guy who had graduated from the UCSF Med School in just 18 months with the highest grades in the school's history.

"C'mon Peter, this is for Rita, she's the human interest reporter." Cathy wasn't at all keen on the idea of spending time on a story about a Med School graduate. "Look," Peter continued, "it says he is a former ball player for the L.A. Rangers, I think I remember him, Chase Hartley, anyway, check it out." Cathy knew when it was fruitless to argue with Peter so she reluctantly returned to her desk to "check it out."

Her computer search revealed what had been on the newswire. Chase Hartley, Thirty one years old former S.F. Rangers player entered Med School at age twenty nine and graduated in eighteen months. Remarkable, but not necessarily newsworthy, Cathy thought as she continued her search. She noted the report of a serious motorcycle accident prior to attending Med School. She wondered if it was the hospital stay that convinced him to become a doctor. She gathered her purse and headed over to UCSF to see what she could learn.

As she drove, Cathy mused over her situation. It was ten years since she graduated from Northwestern with a degree in Journalism. She had hoped to land a job as a TV anchor, but her TV appearances thus far had only been as an investigative reporter for the Times and its TV outlet, WKOX in San Jose. She was beginning to wonder if it was worth the aggravation of uprooting her life and moving from city to city with the broken relationships that it inevitably entailed. The last move from Moline was particularly painful, she had begun thinking that she might forgo her career and settle down in Moline with Matthew, but when the San Jose opportunity came up, she knew she had to give it at least one more shot. She and Matthew had drifted apart, despite their protestations to the contrary. Maintaining a relationship across two thousand miles just didn't happen.

UCSF was very little help in providing her with information on Chase Hartley. They could only give her the name and address of the facility where he was doing his residency; NSCT Research Foundation. She located the facility just north of Half Moon Bay. It was an impressive building that overlooked the Pacific Ocean. Not a bad place to work, she thought as she entered the glass enclosed lobby and approached the receptionist. It seemed strange that there was none of the usual furniture in the lobby.

"Could I see Dr. Hartley," she asked. "May I see your credentials," the woman said. She assumed she meant her drivers' license and her Times ID, but she said "I'm sorry we can only admit persons who have credentials issued by the foundation. “Can I talk to him on the phone?” She asked. “What's your name and the nature of your interest?” She wanted to know. “I’m a reporter with the San Jose Times and I would like to interview him regarding his Med School experience.”

The receptionist made a call and said “You can use this phone,” and handed her one of the phones on her desk. “Dr. Hartley?” Cathy asked. “Yes, how can I help you?” was the reply. “I would like to interview you regarding your Med School experiences,” she said, “Could you suggest a time and place, it should only require about an hour at the most?” “I’m sorry,” he replied, but I don’t do interviews.” “But it would,” she started to say when he interrupted her. “I’m sorry, but as I said, I don’t do interviews, good bye.” And he hung up.

How rude, she thought. “Excuse me, what does the acronym NSCT stand for?” she addressed the receptionist. “Nuclear Somatic Cell Transfer.” “O-------------K, Thank you,” She said, and headed for her car.

On the drive back to San Jose, Cathy thought, I have to hand it to Peter, he smelled a story here and I think he was right. She put in “Nuclear Somatic Cell Transfer” on her smart phone and learned it was a technique for cloning embryos for use in reproductive cloning, in other words, human cloning. Now she understood all the security measures and why they didn't want people snooping around the NSCT Research Foundation.

When she returned to her desk, she was determined to find out everything she could about ball player/doctor Chase Hartley. She found a myriad of items posted up to the time of his accident but nothing afterward. The accident was described as life-threatening with brain damage. His physician, Dr. Brent Alswerp, had called in a Dr. James Barnett from Chicago to perform the surgery.

Dr. Alswerp, she learned, was considered the top brain surgeon on the west coast. Why would he call in a doctor from Chicago? Then she found it. Dr. Alswerp himself had brain surgery the day before Chase Hartley's operation and died on the operating table. The surgeon that performed the surgery on Dr. Alswerp was none other than Dr. James Barnett.

It's amazing, Cathy thought, just a few years ago she would have spent hours in the library archives to learn what she can extract in minutes from the internet.

Cathy pushed back from her desk and stared into space. Something must tie this all together, but what? A common thread here was Dr. James Barnett of Chicago. She determined to talk to him but she knew Peter would never approve the expense for her to fly to Chicago with no promise of a story. Then it struck her, she was scheduled to attend her ten year reunion at Northwestern next month so she should be able to find enough time to track down Dr. Barnett while she was there.

She set out to find everything she could about her quarry. He was a member of the highly regarded surgical partnership of Lindahl, Martin and Barnett. Most surgeries were performed at the Chicago Trinity Hospital. He lived on the 92nd floor of the John Hancock Center in Chicago and he was an avid sailor. The articles noted that he sailed every weekend out of the Belmont Harbor Yacht Club. That should be the best place to try to intercept him, she thought. Based on his graduation dates, she figured he must be about thirty five years old, but she found no mention of a Mrs. Barnett. She devised a plan.

"Dr. Barnett," Janet's voice crackled over the speaker phone, "there is a Cathy Nichols from California on the line and she would like to talk to you. She said it has to do with Dr. Alswerp." "Alright, put her through, Janet," he said.

"Thank you for taking my call, Dr. Barnett, I would like to talk to you about a memorial we are planning for the hospital to honor Dr. Alswerp. I will be in Chicago on Saturday, the 26th and if you could spare me a few minutes I can explain the details. I know you were a good friend to Dr. Alswerp and I felt you would want to be included."

"I have a sailboat race on the 26th at Belmont Harbor," He said."Not a problem, I can meet with you at Belmont after your race. It will only take a few minutes," she pleaded. "Alright, I'll see you then," he said, he thought a memorial was hardly appropriate, but he couldn't tell her that, and because he was known as a close friend of Brent's, he couldn't very well dismiss her.

Chapter Thirteen:

Cathy's reunion date finally arrived and she spent two days renewing friendships and enjoying the festivities, but on Saturday she slipped out early and went back to her hotel to get ready to meet Dr. Barnett. She put on her most appealing dress, a silk like material in a size 4 which exposed just the right amount of her attractive body. She looked in the mirror at her reflection. The colors in the dress highlighted her green eyes and auburn hair. "Not too shabby," she thought, and headed over to the Belmont Harbor Yacht Club. The club was built on a very large floating barge and she had to cross over a ships gangplank to enter. The first deck was used for shower rooms and sail lockers for the members' boats. A large open stairway led to the second deck. Dr. Barnett had said to meet him at the club bar on the upper deck. She climbed the stairs to the upper level. Large picture windows provided a panoramic view of the boats in the harbor and Lake Michigan beyond. The boats were just coming in so she had to wait for about a half hour for Dr. Barnett to show up. Since she wasn't a member, she couldn't buy a drink for herself, so she just waited. She asked the bartender to point out Dr. Barnett to her when he arrived. It wasn't long before the sailors were off their boats and pouring into the bar. She saw the bartender speak to one of them and motioned toward her, indicating that this was Dr. Barnett.

She stood up and started toward the bar, at the same time, he started toward her. He was tall and slender, about six feet two Cathy thought. His clothes were wet and his dark hair was poking out from under his cap, his blue eyes sparkled through beads of perspiration. His sun glasses were hanging around his neck and his welcoming smile made Cathy feel at ease. "Damn," she thought, "this is one attractive man." "You must be Ms. Nichols," he said as he held out his hand. He hoped it was Miss and not Mrs. Please call me Cathy, she said. She was beautiful, he thought as he led her back to the bar. He liked the way her dress clung to her breasts, exposing just enough to attest to their authenticity. "My crew and I are celebrating with a round of Thunderheads, would you like one?" She looked into his eyes, "I don't know, would I?" she repeated his question as if to say, what is a Thunderhead? "It's a drink they came up with here at the club, it's in a tall glass, basically a Tom Collins, but then they pour an ounce and a half of dark Meyers Rum on top, hence, the Thunderhead." She watched as the bartender mixed a row of them for Dr. Barnett and his crew. She saw why they called them Thunderheads, the dark rum settled on the top of the glass in a dark cloud.

They picked up their drinks and Dr. Barnett slipped his arm around her waist and guided her toward a table. He felt her body moving under the silk like fabric of her dress. This is a desirable woman, he thought. "Call me James, Cathy," he said as they sat down. "Great race, skipper," a crew member said, "Hear, hear," the others chimed in. Other skippers and crew stopped by the table to congratulate them. It was somewhat hectic and boisterous. The Thunderheads disappeared quickly. "One more?" he asked. "I think I had better stick with this one," she said, already feeling the effects from the power of devil rum, "but thank you." It was a fun, friendly atmosphere and she was having a good time, almost forgetting what she was there for. After a while things settled down and James said "Listen, I'm sorry we haven't had a chance to talk, and I have to shower and change. There's a great restaurant not far from here, The Hacienda Del Sol, they have excellent Mexican food. If you like, we can go there after I change and we can talk then." "That would be very nice," Cathy said.

James and Peter, one of his crew, left the table and headed for the locker room. "So tell me James, is this Cathy the current "flavor of the month?" Peter asked as they descended the stairs. "No Peter, she is here from California to talk to me about a memorial for a dear friend of mine who passed away recently." "Oh, too bad James, she looks like a cut above your usual fare." "Thanks a lot, Peter," James replied.

When James reappeared at the top of the stairway, Cathy thought her heart would stop. Dressed now in a blue blazer over a white shirt open at the neck, Dr. Barnett was a stunning vision. The blazer accentuated the deep blue in his eyes. As he approached her, he must have sensed the feelings churning inside her, "Are you alright Cathy?" "Yes, yes," she replied. "Great, let's head over to the Hacienda."

He put out his hand and Cathy stood up, facing him, looking into his eyes. She could sense a growing mutual attraction with this intriguing man. When they reached the parking lot she wasn't at all surprised when he helped her into a vintage Jaguar roadster. "Nice car," she remarked. "It's an XK 140 drop head coupe," he said. It was a perfect evening for an open car, but as the wind buffeted her hair, Cathy thought "I'm going to look like a witch by the time we get to the restaurant."

Dr. Barnett didn't seem to notice Cathy's' hair as he helped her out of the Jag at the Hacienda Del Sol. The maitre d' greeted them, "Good evening Dr. Barnett, table for two? The restaurant had tables surrounding a large fountain in the central area and secluded booths on the periphery. A very romantic setting, Cathy thought. They were ushered to a booth by the maitre d'. "Thank you Manuel," Dr. Barnett said as he slipped a bill into Manuel's hand. "Enjoy your dinner," Manuel said with a knowing look and a sound of assurance in his voice as they settled into the booth.

"They make a dynamite Margarita, it is hand mixed with fresh squeezed lemons and limes. Would you like one?" he asked. "How could I refuse," Cathy replied. When the waiter arrived, he ordered two Margaritas with salt, on the rocks, and a Chili con Queso appetizer. They brought the Chili con Queso in a miniature chafing dish surrounded by tortilla chips. The melted cheese and chili mixture was a perfect complement to the Margaritas. Cathy was feeling as soft as the Queso; her attraction to James Barnett was overwhelming her. She had never experienced an evening with the emotion she was feeling now. The conversation became personal, "Tell me Cathy," Dr. Barnett said, holding her left hand in his and stroking her naked ring finger, "Why is it that a woman as desirable as you is still unattached?" She resisted the temptation to say it was none of his business, "Well, Dr. Barnett," she began, "Please Cathy," he interrupted "It's James, remember?" "Yes, I remember," Cathy replied, she had held on to the formality of addressing him as Dr. Barnett to try and maintain her emotional distance. She could feel those barriers crumbling as he held her hand and waited for an answer.

"Well, James," she said, "I think it was a combination of the demands of my career and not having met the person I wanted to share the rest of my life with. But what about you, James, your hand seems to be similarly devoid of jewelry." "My story is strikingly similar to yours, Cathy." James said as he thought; is she the one? Cathy thought; is he the one?

Cathy tried to focus on her mission, "I understand you studied under Dr. Alswerp and were very close to him," "I'd rather not talk about that right now," James said as he put his arm around her and pulled her gently toward him. Cathy offered no resistance and let her body come up tightly to his. He removed his arm and they finished their Chili con Queso and their second Margarita, enjoying the special moment they were sharing, their arms and legs brushing against each other. "Would you like to see the lights of the city from the 92nd floor of the Hancock Building?" He asked. "Is that like: do you want to come up and see my etchings?" she replied. James laughed, "Well, do you?" "Yes, let's go," she said. James motioned to the waiter, "Would you like to order dinner now?" he asked. "No, we'll be leaving now, just bring the check please."

They stepped outside into a balmy Chicago evening. It was a short drive to the Hancock Building, and Cathy enjoyed the wind in her hair this time. When they approached the building, James turned into the parking area and entered a spiral ramp not much wider than the car. Up and up and up they went, James obviously enjoyed putting the Jaguar through its paces until they reached the eighth floor. They could sell tickets for that ride, Cathy thought.

They took an elevator to the 44th floor and had to transfer to another elevator for the trip the rest of the way. When the elevator began to stop, Cathy felt like she was floating in the air. She had to hold onto James to keep from losing her balance. They walked arm and arm to the apartment. The 92nd floor was the top, only TV stations and a restaurant were above. James opened the door and followed her inside. She waited while he closed the door and turned toward her. Neither spoke as they came together, clutching each other eagerly, as if they had waited their entire lives for this moment. James arms encircled her, pulling her firm buttocks against him. She hugged him back, feeling his manliness growing between them. Cathy raised her head and found James mouth with her lips. They kissed feverishly, searching the depths with their tongues. Cathy pulled back, "What are we doing, James, are we ready to commit to where this is headed?" She could tell by his expression that he was as conflicted as she.

She steadied herself against the wall as she went up the steps to the living room. The city's lights spread out before her. A mix of blue, green and orange lights flickered all the way to the horizon. It was a breathtaking sight. She loved the way the lights on Lake Shore Drive carved out the shape of the Lake Michigan shoreline as they disappeared in the distance. James came up behind her, "That glow to the north is Milwaukee, Wisconsin," he said as he came up behind her but he was not really interested in the view. His arms encircled her. His fingers were sending pleasure signals to his brain as they slipped over the contours of her body as he held her against him. She felt his manliness once again, now in the small of her back. She put her hands behind her and pulled him tightly against her. He slid his hands down on top of her dress. He loved the feel of her supple body under the silky fabric. His hands pressed lightly on her sensitive areas as she moved slowly back and forth. She moved side to side against the bulge in his pants. She was crazy with desire. She wanted to spin around and release his throbbing manliness from its captivity, but she couldn't.

"I can't do this James, I can't do it. I came here under false pretenses. I wanted to gain information from you about Chase Hartley. The Alswerp memorial was a fabrication to get to you. Believe me James, I want you right now more than anything, but it's not right. I can understand if you hate me, but in a few short hours I have fallen for you." She felt tears welling in her eyes and started to cry. "Please call me a cab James. I need to go back to my hotel now." The hurt and confused look on his face made her feel worse. He hadn't said a word since her outburst and she felt terrible about hurting him. The doorman called and said the cab was there. James escorted Cathy to the lobby and helped her in the cab. "Bye," he said. "I'm sorry, James, I am so sorry." He closed the car door without further word and went back into the lobby. As he reached the elevator he stopped, "Damn," he thought, "Why did I let her get away?" He ran back through the lobby to the door, but the cab was gone and the street was deserted. He slumped back against the door frame. He felt as empty as the street.

On the flight back to San Jose, Cathy thought about the fiasco in Chicago. She really had fallen for James and she regretted missing out on what certainly would have been a night of passionate love making. She began imagining what might have happened. The further she delved into her scenario, the more upset she became. Why didn't she just let it happen, what an idiot, she would have been burdened with guilt, but the gnawing feeling in the pit of her stomach would have been satiated.

Chapter Fourteen:

“How was the reunion?” Peter asked when she returned to her desk on Monday. “Oh, it was interesting,” she answered. “Yeah, those things usually are.” He responded. You don’t know the half of it, she thought. “What’s happening with that genius doctor story? Peter asked. “Nothing there,” she replied.

Cathy was determined to find out why Chase Hartley and the NSCT were so afraid of publicity. She contacted UCSF and requested a copy of Chase Hartley’s research thesis. She had to invoke the “Freedom of Information Act” before they would agree to release it to her. Although it was packed with theoretical technical analysis, she couldn’t put it down.

The title, “The Scientific, Ethical and Moral Considerations of Human Cloning,” aptly described its contents. He presented evidence of what he described as a “breakthrough” in the success/failure rate in cloning. Based on an automated process for reprogramming the somatic cell nucleus that he developed, the success rate for viable embryos was increased from only 11 percent to over 97 percent. He concludes that at this success rate, human cloning was practical.

Ethical considerations, according to Hartley, should only apply to clones that develop serious illnesses or deformities.

The nature of cloning is such that these problems cannot be avoided, and society will have to institutionalize these clones or euthanize them. Hartley acknowledges that society generally believes that only God can create life, and he offers no solution to how this view can be reconciled with life created by NSCT.

Cathy read and reread Chase's thesis. She understood the high level of security at NSCT. She was sure they were involved in human cloning, which was illegal in California. She was determined to expose what was going on in Half Moon Bay, if, in fact, it involved human cloning. She decided to keep this story to herself, because if Peter knew about it he would assign a team to work on it and she would probably not be a part of the team.

Cathy wondered about James, "Damn," she thought, if only I hadn't messed up so badly. She would lie awake at night thinking about what she would do if she ever got another chance.

She looked for a connection to NSCT Research Foundation from suppliers, subsidiaries, branch offices, customers and employment agencies. She came up with nothing, but one day while she was sitting at her desk suffering through her monthly cramps, it struck her. If, in fact, they are doing human cloning, they need fertile eggs.

She started searching the internet for sites seeking female eggs and for surrogate mothers. Once created, the egg would have to be implanted into a woman who would carry it to term.

Cathy tracked down every lead she found, but had no success until she received a response from an internet site she had contacted seeking a surrogate mother. She had to submit a mountain of personal information before they revealed their interest. If selected, they told her, she would have to submit to a complete physical examination and travel to Arizona for the implant. She finally felt like she was on the right track, for Arizona was one of the few states that did not specifically ban human cloning. She did not want to be impregnated, but she knew she would have to go along with the program if she was to learn anything useful.

She was accepted and asked to take an exam in San Francisco. It was the most excruciating experience of her life. Her visits to the gynecologist were nothing compared to the tests and probing for this exam. She was told that they would be in touch with her. A week later, she received a phone call. They were sending her a ticket to fly to Kingman, Arizona. She would receive $10,000.00 when she was impregnated and signed a confidentiality agreement and $10,000.00 when the baby was born.

She was given a date and time for the flight to Kingman. She decided it was time to bail out of this operation and told them she had a change of heart and could not go through with it. They were very independent and said she would have to pay $875.00 for the exam they had given her. Good luck, she thought. Considering the type of operation they were running, she was sure they did not want to take her to court.

She decided to make a trip to Kingman to see what she could learn. Her inquiries around town yielded nothing. No one had heard of NSCT or of any clinic. She reasoned there must be others like herself that had been flown in to the airport, so she camped out at the airport. Finally she noticed an unmarked van that was picking up a young woman so she decided to follow. It led her to the clinic, about a mile and a half north of town on state road 93.

There were several buildings in the compound surrounded by a large chain link fence. The fence looked like the kind they have around a prison, with barbed wire at the top, slanting inward. They obviously didn't want anyone to leave without permission. There was no sign identifying the facility and she didn't see anyone outside the buildings. She continued down the road when the bus pulled in. She thought about pulling into the gate to see what she could learn, but they probably recorded the license numbers of anyone pulling in to the gate.

A few miles up the road she turned around and headed back to Kingman. She stopped at the first business she found. It was a small diner with an EAT sign on a pole by the road. The place was empty except for the man behind the counter. "Howdy," he said. "Howdy," she responded as she climbed on a stool. “What can I get for you Miss?” “Just a cup of coffee,” she answered.

Cathy looked up and down the empty counter and said,”Business a little slow today?” “Every day,” came the answer. “I would think you would get a lot of customers from that Clinic up the road,” she said. “Nope, in fact they’re the reason my business is so bad. No one goes in or out of that place except on their bus. It goes by here once or twice a day on trips into town, but it never stops. People are afraid of that place, nobody knows what goes on in there and nobody wants to get too close.”

“Please keep my card, and if you see or hear anything from there please give me a call.” Cathy decided to look up the owner of the clinic site parcel at the Mohave County Courthouse. The Arizona Land Trust was the owner of record. To learn who was behind the Arizona Land Trust she would have to contact the Secretary of State in Phoenix. She drove back to San Jose and sent a request to Mohave County for the filing record of the Arizona Land Trust. The response was not surprising. NSCT Research Foundation was one of those listed as a beneficial owner.

Chapter Fifteen:

"Dr. Barnett?"

"Yes Janet"

"There is a process server in the lobby asking for you."

"OK, send him in."

"Dr. James Barnett?"

"Yes, that's me."

"Here you are sir," he said as he handed Dr. Barnett the papers.

James looked at the papers and immediately noted the name, Henry Alswerp. He was not surprised by the service, but a feeling of foreboding overtook him. He glanced at the papers, "Death of Dr. Brent Alswerp," "Malpractice." He was shocked and saddened by what he saw. He had more or less expected Brent's brother to file a suit, but being served with the papers confirmed his fears. He hoped Ann wouldn't be dragged into the unpleasantness that may lie ahead.

"Janet, please call the attorneys for our insurance company and let them know we are sending this over, and also see if you can find a current number for Chase Hartley."

James dialed the number that Janet had found for Chase. "NSCT Research Foundation," said a pleasant woman's voice. "Dr. Chase Hartley," he said, not really knowing if he was in the right place.

It was with a sense of relief when the voice said "One moment please."

"This is Dr. Hartley," "Chase," he said "James Barnett." "Hey, James, how are you, it's been a long time." "I know, sorry Chase, after your graduation we pretty much lost touch. How have you been? What are you doing now?"

"I'm busier than the proverbial paper hanger, James, but what prompts your call?"

"Not good news, I'm afraid," James said, "Henry Alswerp is suing me for malpractice in the death of Dr. Brent Alswerp.

"Oh no," Chase said, "I can't imagine what basis he thinks justifies that charge."

"I don't know either, Chase, but justification is not always a requisite for these actions."

"Yeah, right," Chase said, "Listen James, could you have your secretary send me whatever correspondence you receive on this case? I'll give her my address if you can get her on the line."

"Sure Chase, we'll talk more when you have time."

James was familiar with the drill, although he had never been found at fault; he had been required to defend himself in several cases. The interrogatories would be first, followed by depositions and then the trial itself unless the insurance company settled. He wondered what they might have in the form of evidence upon which to base a lawsuit. All this would come out in the depositions and the interrogatories, he was certain of that.

"Tom Andrews from Andrews and McInerny is on the line," Janet said. James took the call. "James, Tom here, we will have to hand off that lawsuit you sent over regarding a Dr. Brent Alswerp. It was filed in California and we aren't licensed to practice there. There is a firm there that works for the company. We have used them in the past and had good luck. We will be referring this case to them." "I don't suppose we have a lot of choice," James said.

"I will send them a copy of the suit and ask them to give you a call." "Thanks Tom, I'll look for their call." James was uneasy, he had worked with Tom's firm and felt a level of comfort with them, but he was concerned about having to work with a California firm he didn't know, especially on this case.

Soon he did receive a call. "This is Larry Pusiteri of Pusiteri, Hendricks and Belcher, the caller said. Tom Andrews referred your case to us." "Yes, I was expecting your call, how do we proceed from here?" he asked. Larry explained that their charges would initially be paid by the insurance company and he would be sending interrogatories, taking depositions and representing him at the trial, if it reached that point. "We will schedule the depositions for your convenience," he said, "But we will be at the mercy of the court regarding the trial dates." "I understand," James said.

When he received the first set of interrogatories he could discern the approach the plaintiffs seemed to be taking. Beside the usual name, address, phone number, etc., they wanted the names of all those present during any discussions connected with Dr. Alswerp's operation. List all those present at the operation. What was the purpose of the operation? Who consented to the operation? All data connected to Dr. Alswerp's illness, and on and on.

A few weeks after he returned the interrogatories, he heard from Larry Pusiteri, "The plaintiff's attorneys' have scheduled depositions for Dr. Andrew Nerneau and Margaret White, RN. They have asked to take yours on May 6th or June 13th. Are either of those dates OK with you?" James checked his calendar. "I can be there on May 6th," He replied.

Depositions always made him nervous, and James was uneasy as he rode the elevator to the 35th floor of The Pyramid Center. Larry met him at the reception area, "Dr. Barnett, I'm pleased to meet you, glad you could make it. Let me brief you on what to expect; they have deposed Dr. Nerneau and nurse White and they have stated under oath that you removed a section of Dr. Alswerp's brain and had it placed in a preservation vessel." The company has not made a settlement offer until they review your deposition. Larry ushered him into the conference room where the deposition would be taken. Seated around a large table were the plaintiffs' attorneys, a court reporter and another attorney from Larry's firm.

"Please be seated, Dr. Barnett," the attorney introduced everyone and the court reporter administered the oath. After an endless stream of questions which seemed to be completely unrelated to the case, they finally asked one that made sense. "What was the purpose of the operation Dr. Barnett.?" "The purpose of the operation was to remove and preserve Dr. Alswerp's brain." James stated. "Can we have a short recess?" the attorney asked. "Certainly," Larry replied.

When they reached the hallway outside the conference room, Larry said,"They weren't ready for that answer Dr. Barnett. In the previous depositions the purpose was described as an exploratory operation to determine the extent of damage caused by the CJD."

When they reconvened, their first question was, "Dr. Barnett, you said the purpose of the operation was to remove the brain of Dr. Alswelp, is that correct?" "Yes it is," James replied. "Why would you perform such an operation, Dr. Barnett, did you not take a Hippocratic Oath when you received your medical degree?" "Yes I did," James replied. "Can you recite that oath, Dr.?" "No?" "Let me refresh your memory, 'I will practice for the good of my patients, and avoid harming them,'"

"Do you think you harmed Dr. Alswerp by removing his brain?" "No, I don't" James replied. "Dr. Alswerp was rapidly succumbing to a debilitating disease, he had only weeks to live and wanted his brain to be preserved for the future. He asked me, actually pleaded with me to perform the operation. If you refer to the authorization he signed for the operation, you will see it calls for a 'radical craniectomy.' When I received notice of this lawsuit, I checked the recording made in the operating room and when Dr. Alswerp was asked to state the procedure he was to receive, he replied, 'radical craniectomy'." "A radical craniectomy is of course, the complete removal of the patients' brain, and this is exactly what we did." James stated emphatically.

The attorneys seemed flustered, "Off the record, please," he instructed the court reporter. "Do we have a copy of the authorization Dr. Alswerp signed?" he asked. His assistant shuffled through a stack of papers and came up with it. "How did we miss this?" he asked his fellow attorney, pointing to the statement on the authorization describing the operation. The attorney was chagrined, "I don't know," he answered." "Back on the record please," he said to the reporter, "We will need a copy of this recording of the operating room that Dr.Barnett described. James stated his agreement to provide the recording. "I think we are finished for now," the attorney looked at James' attorney,

"Do you have any questions for your client?" "No." "Good, then, this deposition is ended."

James attorney met with him in the reception area after the others had left. "They are clearly flustered by the authorization and the recording," he said. "I must admit I also didn't catch the significance of the 'radical craniectomy' when I reviewed the paperwork." "Thanks for making the trip, James," Larry said, "I'll let you know what I hear from them, but at this point, I don't think they have a case and we don't intend to offer a settlement."

Less than a week later, Larry called. "James, I have some good news and some bad news." "The good news is they are dropping the case against you. The bad news and I'm afraid it is really bad, is they are turning over their documentation to the State Attorney's Office for possible criminal prosecution."

"Criminal prosecution for what?" James asked. "Well, Larry went on, they feel that what you did amounted to assisted suicide and as you know, that is illegal in California. Even in Oregon, where it is legal, it must be accomplished 'hands off' by the physician with the patient administering the deadly potion themselves." I'm really sorry, James, this can turn out to be a very serious matter for you. Let's hope they decide not to proceed against you. We won't be able to represent you on this James, because I think you know your policy doesn't cover willful or illegal acts by the physician. If the States Attorney does proceed against you, I can recommend some very good criminal lawyers." "Thanks," James said. This is great, he thought, out of the frying pan, into the fire. He really didn't like the idea of having to deal with another group of lawyers, especially when it involved criminal charges.

James called Chase to tell him the news about the lawsuit. "James, nice to hear from you, how is the lawsuit coming along?"

"Well, today I received the proverbial good news-bad news. They dropped the lawsuit, but they turned over their documentation to the States Attorney General for possible prosecution for assisted suicide." "Oh my God," Chase was shocked. "Do you think they will proceed? If you hear from them, be sure and let me know right away." "Will do," James replied.

"Listen James; are we on a secure phone line?" Chase wanted to know. "Yes we are," James said. "OK, I have some fantastic news. I have isolated the wave modulation of Alpha frequency brain waves and locked in on their characteristics. It is similar to how a modem unscrambles signals. I have done it James! I have done it! My associates aren't even aware of what I have accomplished so you must not mention this to anyone. The next time you come out here I will show you how this works. I couldn't be more excited James, I think this is what He had in mind for me all along. This is the first step in being able to transfer cranial content in a non-invasive procedure."

“Chase, that is incredible, I can’t wait to see it. I’ll definitely call you when I head out there.”

“Good luck James.”

“Thanks Chase.”

Chapter Sixteen:

It didn't take long! "Dr. Barnett," Janet's voice came in on his speaker phone. "Yes Janet," "There are two detectives here from the Chicago Police Department. They say they have a California warrant for your arrest." "I'll be right out, Janet." He said and thought "Damn, this sounds like trouble." He came out of his office to meet the two men who were waiting for him. If he were casting a detective show, the two would be perfect he thought. One was tall and lanky and the other was stout and burly.

"Are you Dr. James Barnett?" the burly one asked. "Yes, I am." "Are you the Dr. James Barnet that performed an operation on a Dr. Brent Alswerp?" "Yes, again," he said. "We have a warrant for your arrest. You will have to come with us. We have orders to hold you for extradition on a San Francisco indictment." That said, the lanky one produced a pair of handcuffs and said, "Please put your hands out." James thought, this can't be happening, what about an attorney? What about my rights? Can they just waltz in here and cart me off? "What am I charged with?" James wanted to know. "Second degree murder," was the response in chorus.

"Ok, let's go sir," the burly one said. They took him to the elevator and down to their police car for his ride to the Cook County Jail. When they arrived, he was "booked," fingerprinted and issued an orange jail garment. He was allowed one phone call and he used it to call Larry Pusiteri. "Mr. Pusiteri is on the other line," the woman said, "can I have him call you back?" "No, I have to talk to him now, I only get one call and this is it." "Who can I say is calling?" "It's Dr. Barnett and I am at the county jail." "Just a minute," she said. Larry Pusiteri came on the line, "James, what happened?" "The Chicago Police arrested me for the murder of Dr. Alswerp. They are holding me for extradition to California," he said.

True to their word, detectives from the California States Attorneys' Office arrived and escorted him on the airplane to the county jail in San Francisco, California.

"You have a visitor," the guard said, and ushered him to the visitor area. "Dr. Barnett?" He was a large man with a friendly but stern countenance, James was pleased, I can work with this man, he thought. "I'm Sherman Burck of Burck, Jantzen and Potter, you can call me Sherman. Larry Pusiteri called me and explained your situation. I'll be representing you this morning at the arraignment if that is your wish." "Yes, thank you," James said.

"How do you intend to plead?" Sherman asked. "What options do I have?" James asked. "You can plead "Guilty," "Not guilty," "No contest" or "Mute." Sherman said. "I'm familiar with "Guilty" and "Not guilty," James said, "but what happens if I plead "No contest" or "Mute?"

"Well," Sherman began, and James could sense that he had explained these pleas more times than he would like to remember. A plea of "No contest" means you do not admit guilt, but you do not dispute the charges." A "Mute" plea means you stand mute and do not enter a plea. The court will then enter a "not guilty" plea for you. By standing mute, you avoid admitting to the correctness of the proceedings against you up to that point."

"Sounds like I should enter a "Mute" plea, unless there is something I'm missing, James said.

"Mute" it is," Sherman agreed.

"When I looked into your case this morning, I found they have already arraigned two others on the same charge, Dr. Andrew Nerneau and Margaret White. They have both bonded out. I am going to ask the Judge to release you on your own recognizance." True to his word, James was released on personal recognizance and he was a free man once again that morning. He did have to report to the District Attorney in Chicago on a weekly basis, but he was free. He did not have to return to California until the pre-trial conference in two weeks. He believed Sherman Burck had been successful on his behalf up to this point.

James and his attorney met at the courthouse with Margaret and Andrew and their attorneys prior to the pre-trial conference. "I have been reviewing the depositions you gave in connection with the malpractice lawsuit, and to be honest with you, I don't see much to work with here in regard to your defense," Sherman said, and continued, "I know the prosecutor and the judge are not anxious for this case to go forward and I think we can get a very favorable plea deal on these charges. "No way," James said. "Don't be too quick to dismiss the idea James," Dr. Nerneau said, "what kind of a deal do you think we could get?" he asked. "Maximum sentence for this crime," Sherman continued, "if you are found guilty, is life in prison." Furtive glances were exchanged between James and Andrew and Margaret. Until now, none of them had realistically faced the situation they now found themselves in.

"Excuse me James, I need to meet with the Judge now," Sherman said, and he along with Margaret and Andrews' attorneys filed into the Judge's chambers. They were met by the District Attorney and introduced to the Judge. The district attorney presented his evidence for the charges, based primarily on the statements made from the depositions previously made for the malpractice lawsuit. When he finished presenting the evidence, the judge asked Sherman and the other attorneys if they wanted to present any evidence to refute what had been presented. "Nothing at this time, Your Honor," They replied. The Judge turned to the District Attorney, "Have there been any discussions regarding a plea deal in this case?" "Not at this time, Your Honor," he replied. "I will set another conference three weeks from today to give you time to work out a plea deal if one is possible," he said.

James did some serious soul searching on the plane ride back to Chicago. He hadn't seen this coming when he agreed with Brent to perform the operation. He understood how the District Attorney could view the case as "assisted suicide", but he wondered how did it get to murder? It was an operation of mercy. Mercy for a man who wanted to continue the important work he had devoted his life to. James knew his best defense would require testimony from Brent/Chase, but he, along with Dr. Nerneau and Margaret had made a solemn promise of secrecy to Brent when he pleaded with them to form a pact of silence. He wasn't sure how to defend himself and hoped Sherman could provide some help.

"Sherman Burck on the line," Janet announced over the speaker phone.

"James, I have some good news, the prosecutor has asked the Judge to agree to a plea deal that would involve two to five years with possible parole in 18 months." I think Dr. Nerneau and Ms. White are going to accept the deal. I talked to their attorneys and they are in favor of it. How do you feel about the plea deal James?"

How do I feel? James thought. He didn't want to spend two years in jail, that's for sure.

"I don't think I could go along with it," James said. "You do realize that if you go to trial and lose, you could spend the rest of your life in jail." Sherman said. "Yes I do," James replied.

"If you want to fight this James, they will split your case from the others,"

"So be it," James replied.

Sherman arranged a meeting with Dr. Nerneau, Margaret and their attorneys at the courthouse prior to their conference with the judge. "As you know," he began, "the prosecution and the Judge have agreed to a plea deal and Andrew and Margaret have accepted. Do you still feel you want to go to trial on this charge James?" "Yes I do," James answered.

Andrew looked directly at James, "You know you could be facing prison for the rest of your life? He said, his voice rising, "We don't have a viable defense, James please think it over, 18 months or life." James turned to Margaret, "how do you feel about it Margaret?" "I don't know James, I haven't slept much in the past few months, worrying about this, but I think I agree with Andrew, I just can't face the thought of spending the rest of my life in prison." James put his hand on her shoulder. "I understand, Margaret," He said.

"It's time for our conference," Sherman said, "And James, we'll meet afterwards to discuss our case." They all followed Sherman into the courtroom. The district attorney's people were waiting for them. The clerk left to notify the Judge that everyone was present. The Judge appeared and listened as the charge was read, "The Superior Court of the City of San Francisco versus Dr. James Barnett, Dr. Andrew Nerneau and Ms. Margaret White, RN for violation of California Penal Code 401 in the assisted euthanasia of Dr. Brent Alswerp. "I understand there has been some agreement with the prosecution," the Judge said to the District Attorney. "Yes, Your Honor, we have agreed to a sentence of two to five years with possible parole in 18 months if it pleases the court." "Very well, how do the defendants plead?" The Judge asked. Dr. Andrew Nerneau: "Guilty", Your Honor. Ms. Margaret White, RN, "Guilty", Your Honor. Dr. James Barnett, James stood mute. The court enters a plea of "Not Guilty" said the Judge.

Sherman addressed the Judge, "I would ask, Your Honor, that the defendants bail be continued until the trial and sentencing." "Granted, you will be advised of the trial date following discovery."

When they left the courtroom, Sherman and James met in an empty conference room. We can expect a trial date in about eight weeks, but I can stretch that out if you think we need more time," he said. "I have to be honest with you James; the depositions present a pretty strong case against you." "I understand," he said, "but I believe a jury will understand the unique circumstances of this case and acquit me." "I pray you are right," he replied, "I will call you in the next few weeks to set up a meeting to map our strategy."

James found it difficult to concentrate on his work and asked his partners for a leave of absence until the trial was over. He met with Sherman but was unable to provide him with any additional facts that could help his case. As Sherman said, the depositions spoke for themselves and he would have to create an alternative interpretation to create a question of doubt for the jurors. It was only five weeks until his trial. James was apprehensive, he had never faced criminal charges, and with the pledge of secrecy which Brent had insisted on, he had no idea on how to defend himself.

Chapter Seventeen:

There she was, his beloved Adagio, sitting up on blocks looking forlorn and lonely. It hurt him to see her suffering this neglect. The woman at the boat yard office said she thought the boat was listed for sale with Perriman Yacht Brokers. The sales agent at Perriman said that she was indeed listed with their company. He said the boat had just recently been put up for sale after sitting in dry dock for the past two years. The owner, a widow, did not want to sell the boat, but yard bills and insurance costs had convinced her that she had to part with it. Chase arranged to meet the agent at the yard to inspect the boat. As he climbed the ladder to reach the deck, a flood of memories engulfed him. The afternoon sunset sails off the coast, the weekend trips to the Island and the evenings at anchor enjoying a Merlot in the cockpit. Adagio looked pretty much as he had left her. She needed a good cleaning and new paint on her topsides and bottom but that was about it. He made an offer to the agent contingent upon a satisfactory appraisal by a marine surveyor. He arranged for a slip at the Balmar Yacht Club in Corona del Mar and when the survey came in clean as he had anticipated, he launched the boat as soon as the painting was finished and sailed Adagio to her new home.

He was cleaning the cabin one afternoon when he heard a familiar voice. "Ahoy Adagio." He knew that voice. He came up the ladder and peered at the dock, it was Ann. "I don't mean to intrude," she said, "but the agent told me you had brought the boat here and I wanted to see her in the water again and to meet the new owner." He scrambled up on the deck. "Believe me, it is not an intrusion," he said, "Here, let me help you aboard." He reached out his hand to help her climb over the lifeline onto the deck. As she grasped his hand, a look of confusion crossed her face, but quickly evaporated. She looked great. Ann had always been a believer in proper diet and exercise to keep in shape, and the years had been good to her. Her slender body was still firm and supple, and her eyes had an unmistakable twinkle to them. Her short blond hair framed the face of this thirty- something woman in a way that made her smile exude warmth and mystery.

"I must apologize for the condition of the boat, I haven't had time to do a proper cleaning job yet," he said as he retrieved a cushion from the cabin for Ann to sit on. She looked around at the cockpit and rigging and said "She looks just like she did the last time I was aboard." She continued, "In the years since my husband passed away, I haven't wanted to see the boat, there were too many memories to contend with, but when I heard the boat had been bought and returned to the club docks, I felt I had to come and take a look." "I'm so glad you did," he said, "Would you like to take a look around down below?" "Yes, I think I would," she said. He went down the ladder and reached out his hand once again to help her down the steps. "I'm OK, she said as she held onto the stair rails." He didn't think she had yet dealt with the emotions that were stirred up when he helped her aboard. She settled onto the settee where she always would sit when they were in the cabin and looked around at the familiar surroundings. She recognized the music that was playing. "That was my husbands' favorite CD," she said. "Are you a fan of Bobby Hackett?" "It was in the player when I turned it on," he said, "So I thought I would give it a listen, it's called 'Music 'til dawn' do you like it?" he asked. He wondered why he asked the question, because he knew she would only listen to it to please him. He had always enjoyed relaxing to the mellow sounds after a days' sail. "It's alright," she said, "But I must be going, I have already imposed upon you." "No, not at all," he said, "let me offer you a drink, how about a Mt. Gay and lime?" he asked. Ever since their bare boat charter in the Bahamas, where they were introduced to Mt. Gay rum, it had been their drink of choice. They had wanted to see what cruising in the eastern Atlantic waters was like compared to Pacific Ocean cruising. They loved the Caribbean and after spending a week in the islands, they hadn't wanted to leave.

"I don't know, I really don't want to impose, but perhaps just one would be nice," she said. As Chase prepared the drinks, Ann marveled at how he had become so familiar with the boat in such a short time. He seemed to know where everything was without hunting around. He went directly to the 'secret' compartment where Brent had stored the liquor supplies. How did he know it was behind that panel? "Thank you," she said as he handed her the Mt. Gay. "You have a look of puzzlement on your face," he said.

She was startled that he could read her so easily. "I can't get over how much 'at home' you seem to be after being on board for such a short time." "Yes," he said, "it's amazing in a way, but I feel like this boat and I were always meant to be together." He sat down on the settee next to her and raised his glass to hers, "to Adagio" he said.

Ann sipped her Mt. Gay and wondered about the strange connection she felt toward this man whom she had just met. He was young, but still she had this feeling of empathy that she imagined he also shared. When she looked into his eyes, there was a depth to them that drew her ever deeper into him.

"The agent told me your name was Chase Hartley, but that is really all I know about you. Who are you, really, and why do I feel like I've known you forever?" Ann was asking a question that could not be answered.

Chase knew that if he tried to tell Ann the entire story, it would undoubtedly bring her more grief than comfort. He decided to skirt the issue. He put his arm on the back of the couch behind her and replied, "Ann, sometimes a man and woman are brought together whose background and life experiences form a pattern that inexplicably draws them together as one." She was shaken by his reply. She hadn't expected an answer that would strike at the depth of her feelings.

Chase could see she was confused and upset. He took the drink from her hand and set it on the table next to his. He put his arm around her and she moved to him. “I don’t know what is happening,” she said, “but it feels so good, so natural.” She let him pull her up close to him. A feeling of comfort and contentment swept over her. Chase allowed himself the pleasure of feeling her body against his. It had been a long time since he had held her but he could not remember her ever feeling quite this good. His loins were responding and his thoughts immediately turned to taking her to the aft stateroom and making love to her.

Hold on Chase, think about what you are doing, she is fragile right now and doesn’t need her life complicated by a rendezvous with you. Her body was responding to his every movement, no matter how slight. All the signals indicated she wanted him to continue his advances, but Chase wasn’t sure he was reading them correctly. Ann was very sensitive and wore her feelings on her sleeve but she also had a very strong moral code.

He thought he had better try and find out just what she was thinking. “If you don’t mind my asking, how long has it been since your husband die--, uh passed--, uh left you?” She didn’t take offense to the question, “Three years, one month and twelve days.” She said as if she was reciting her name and address. “Have you uh been with anyone during this time?” he asked. “I should tell you that it is none of your business,” she said, “but somehow I don’t object to your question, I have met some very nice men, but I am not ready for a serious relationship.”

He was so glad he had taken this approach. It was clear to him now that although her response to him could have been interpreted to mean she wanted to jump into the bunk with him, this clearly was not the case. She was feeling a connection with him and the empathy of their meeting created an atmosphere where she could bond with him in a spiritual way but she was not looking for a sexual encounter. He took some solace in the fact that she had not been with another man since he 'left'. He couldn't make such a claim. He thought about Sam and a feeling of guilt swept over him. He knew he hadn't had a chance in hell of turning Sam down, but it still made him feel guilty.

"I really must be going now," Ann said, and stood up to leave. "He took her two hands in his, facing her in the cabin, "Would you come for a sail with me some day?" He asked. "I would love to, my number is in the book," she said as she climbed the ladder and went ashore.

Chase wanted to call her the next day, but he didn't want to be too eager, so he waited several days. "Ann, this is Chase, I thought I would take a day sail on Saturday and I was wondering if you might like to ride along." After what seemed an eternity, her reply came, "Yes, that sounds like fun, what time? Shall I meet you at the boat?"

"Yes, that would be great, say 9 o'clock?" he said.

"I'll see you then," she answered.

Chase was exhilarated. He couldn't wait 'til Saturday morning.

"Ahoy Adagio," Ann hailed. "Welcome aboard," Chase said as he climbed up the companionway. Ann handed him a basket as she came aboard. "I brought some sandwiches." "Fantastic," Chase said as he stowed the basket in the cabin. "I haven't changed much on the boat, so you should find things pretty much as they were." "If you're ready, I'll crank up the Perkins and we'll be on our way." Chase said as he started the diesel engine. As always, it fired up on the first crank. "I'll get the stern lines if you can take care of the bow lines," he said.

Ann moved about the boat with the assurance of one with years of experience handling lines and sails. When they cleared the harbor, Chase said "If you will take the wheel, I'll raise the main." Ann steered the boat into the wind so he could raise the main without fighting the wind in the sail. He came back to the cockpit. "You can fall off a little now," he said, as she steered the boat to allow the main sail to fill and start driving the boat. Chase killed the diesel and unfurled the genoa.

The boat came alive, heeling over from the force of the wind and surging through the waves. Chase trimmed the main sheet and sat down next to Ann. She had a light touch on the wheel and was keeping the boat 'on the edge'- not too close to the wind and not too far off the wind. Her face was aglow. "Great work, Ann," Chase said. "This is a great day for sailing, I love it," she replied. "Let's sail to Angel Island for our lunch, I know where there is a delightful private cove." he said. "Sounds good," Ann said. When they entered the harbor, Chase furled the Genoa and Ann brought the boat into the wind so Chase could drop the main sail. Chase went forward and dropped the anchor. Sheltered by the tall trees surrounding the cove, Adagio lay back quietly on her anchor. Ann brought out the sandwiches and Chase uncorked a bottle of Chablis. They sat in the idyllic bosom of the bay and enjoyed their lunch. "I could stay here forever," Ann said wistfully.

They were blessed with the same great weather on the return to their harbor. Chase managed to back the boat into the slip with his usual panic attack and they secured the mooring lines. Adagio was home once again. Ann helped Chase square away the lines and tie on the mainsail cover.

"I think I'll have a Mt. Gay, would you like one?" Chase asked. "That sounds great, I'll fix us a snack," Ann said and headed for the galley. "There's some smoked Gouda in the fridge," Chase said. Ann found the cheese and some crackers and headed back to the cockpit. Chase emerged from the cabin with the drinks. He sat down next to Ann and raised his glass in a toast, "To Adagio," "To Adagio," Ann replied.

They watched the sun setting over the harbor entrance as they enjoyed their Mt. Gay and each other's company. Ann thought about the many times she had enjoyed this experience with Brent. She was just now learning to feel pleasure without a feeling of guilt because Brent wasn't with her to share the joy.

"I really had fun today, thanks for inviting me Chase," Ann said as she got up to gather her things to leave. "Must you go?" Chase asked. "Yes, I'm afraid so," Ann replied. "How about next Saturday?" Chase said, hoping for a yes. "That would be nice, I'll see you here at 9 o'clock," Ann said as she climbed onto the dock.

Ann began to look forward to Saturdays. The weekly sail with Chase had become the focal point of her life. She always had loved sailing, but with Chase, it had become much more. She felt a bond with him that she had only felt once before, with Brent. She and Chase had never made love, but she was sure he shared the intimacy she felt. Although he was quite a bit younger, she believed they had something very special. She found herself imagining what it would be like the day they finally consummated their attraction for each other.

Ann had grown up with the notion that sex was something to be endured, rather than enjoyed. She couldn't remember exactly how she had come to believe that, but she was sure it had influenced her relationship with Brent. She now realized how much enjoyment she had foregone simply because of that long held belief. She regretted her passivity and wished she could have had a second chance with Brent. She determined not to let her misconception spoil her experience if she had the opportunity now. She was eager to explore the possibilities with Chase.

After their Saturday sail, when they were finishing their drinks in the cockpit, Chase put his arm around her and said, "Ann, there is something I have to tell you, I haven't told you before because I didn't want to lose you, but I don't want anything to be between us because you see, I have fallen very much in love with you." "Shortly after your husband died, Dr. Barnett operated on me for brain damage from a motorcycle accident."

"Stop Chase, I don't want to hear it now, I love you too." She put her arms around him and kissed him hard on the mouth. Chase savored her kiss, he really wanted to tell Ann the whole story but he was feeling her lips and her body against his in a way that made him think of only one thing at the moment.

"Come, Ann," he said as he stood up and led her to the companionway. He began unbuttoning her blouse as they approached the aft stateroom. She sat up on the bunk and he leaned her back and kissed her neck and her shoulders. He unsnapped her bra and ran his hands over her breasts, squeezing them gently and biting her nipples. She felt pleasure she hadn't known for years, she put her hands on Chase's head and held it down as he kissed her breasts. This is even better than she had imagined it would be. She had never been so eager for a man, she let go of Chase's head and put her hands between his legs. She found what she wanted, running her hands over his shorts, feeling the growing bulge under her hands. She had wondered if she was 'dried up' and would ever again have an orgasm or feel sexual passion. She now knew the answer to that as she slid off the bunk onto the deck.

Kneeling on the deck, her arms around his legs, she looked up at Chase. He looked down at her with a look that said "yes, please." She found the button on his shorts and unzipped them. She put her hands around his waist and pulled down his underwear with his shorts. His hardness sprang out at her. She ran her hands up and down the inside of his thighs and over his hardness. She cradled his sack in her hands and caressed it as she kissed his body. She put her arms around his bare buttocks and hugged him as she kissed his skin over, under and around his hardness. She was thrilled by the size and stiffness of him as she kissed and fondled it. She wanted to feel him inside her. She stood up and took off her shorts and panties. Chase set her on the edge of the bunk and stood between her legs. He guided his hardness into her very slowly as if he was afraid he would hurt her. He felt the warmth of her sweet juices as they swirled around the head. Ann had never before allowed herself to release the passion she was unleashing now as she felt him hesitate to force himself inside her. She grabbed Chases' buttocks and pulled him tightly against her. She felt her skin against his skin with his hardness buried deeply into her. He pulled back and then slammed against her, harder and harder, faster and faster. Then he stopped, pumping slowly to prolong the pleasure. He didn't want the feeling of being inside her to end too quickly. She looked into his eyes, I love you Chase, her eyes said. She couldn't stand the ecstasy she was feeling, her body was on fire, consuming her. She couldn't hold back an orgasm that was spreading through her from her toes to her head. Chase stopped thrusting, he thrust again, he said "Yes" and he thrust again, "Yes" and again "Yes". He collapsed onto her, motionless, exhausted, their naked bodies together, melded into one. After a while, Chase rolled off of Ann onto his back. "I have never felt anything even close to what I just experienced, that was incredible Ann." She turned on her side and stroked his hair, kissed him and said "Yes it was, Chase, yes it was." I can't wait 'til next week, she thought, maybe they will forgo the sail and spend the entire day making love.

Chapter Eighteen:

Cathy was at her desk, scanning the AP wire when her heart stopped. There, on the wire, Dr. James Barnett was to stand trial for second degree murder in the death of Dr. Brent Alswerp. Two others had pleaded "guilty" in the case and were going to serve two to five years. She thought she might faint; she just wanted to collapse onto her desk and sob. She had tried to block out thoughts of her evening with James, but here he was, on the wire, charged with murder! She wished she could be with him right that minute, holding him, comforting him. This must be excruciating for him. Dr. Alswerp was his mentor and a close friend, and now to be charged with his murder? Cathy couldn't fathom it, I have to go to him, she thought, even if he won't see me. She read on in the release, jury selection was to begin August 12th in Judge Ernest Wilson's courtroom.

She took the wire into Peter's office, "Peter, that story I'm working on about the genius doctor, ex ballplayer?" she began, "Yes, what about it Cathy," "There's a tie-in with this Dr. James Barnett in this release. The operation that saved Chase Hartley's life was performed by James Barnett. I think there is a good story here Peter, and I would like permission to pursue it." "I know you well enough by now Cathy to know better than deny you a story, you always come through, so go for it." "Thank you, Peter"

Jury selections did not usually attract many spectators and there was just a smattering of observers in the courtroom when she arrived. She saw James seated at the table with his attorney and they would converse as each juror was questioned. She could see this would be a long process as most prospects were rejected by his attorney based on answers to questions regarding euthanasia. Judge Wilson decided to continue with the selection the following day and adjourned court.

James and his attorney stood up and turned to come down the aisle. Cathy sat, terrified of what James would say, if anything, when he saw her. As he approached, he glanced in her direction and stopped in his tracks. She stood up and looked him in the eyes. "You," he said. "Yes," was all she could muster. He saw the fear of being rejected in her eyes. "Cathy," James said and reached out to her. She flew into his arms and they stood hugging each other. Cathy was sobbing, she couldn't help herself, she was so happy and relieved. James held her until she stopped sobbing and said "I missed you terribly, girl, please have dinner with me tonight." "I would love to," she said. "Pump Room, Palace Hotel, 8 o'clock?" "I'll be there," she said, happiness overwhelming her, then terror. "Wait, James," he stopped and turned around, "Yes Cathy."

"I didn't plan on staying in town and I'm not dressed for the Pump Room. I don't have time to drive home and change." She hoped he wouldn't say forget it, it's too much trouble.

"I'll meet you in the bar at the Palace at 7 o'clock and we'll figure it out." He said.

Thank you God, she thought. Cathy arrived at the Palace promptly at five minutes to seven. She looked in the bar but she didn't see James anywhere, so she stood outside at the entrance trying not to look as uncomfortable as she felt. She didn't want to have to wait alone in the bar.

"Hey," she turned around, startled, "How did I not see you?" "Sneaky," He said, "come on let's get a table." Cathy thought how different it was from the last time they met. James was so serious, with this huge weight hanging over him. He sensed her feelings, "Not like the last time, is it?" The waiter came for their order. "I'm sure they don't make Thunderheads here," he said, "What would you like?" "Cosmo would be nice," she said. "I'll have a Mt. Gay and lime." He saw her quizzical look and said, "Brent turned me onto them, he and Ann got hooked on them in the Bahamas." When the waiter left they turned their attention back to each other.

"James, I'm so terrified by this, how are you handling it? "It's frightening, sometimes I catch myself wondering what it would be like to spend the rest on my life in prison, but so far I have been able to push those thoughts out of my mind."

"Is there anything I can do to help?" she said, "I do have a few connections, I know I never told you, but I work for the San Jose Times, perhaps there is some way I could help."

"What do you do there?" "I am an investigative reporter." She said. "Well, I don't know of anything you could help with right now, but I can tell you that having you here with me right now gives me peace that I haven't felt for months." "Oh James," she said, as she put her hands on his hands and looked into his eyes, "I don't want to frighten you, but I have to tell you, I love you, James." Cathy knew this was dangerous territory at this stage in a relationship. The quickest way to send someone out the door was to tell them you loved them. James gaze never wavered from hers, "I love you too, Cathy, I know we have only known each other for a matter of hours, but I feel like I've known you all my life, and I love what I see." Encouraged by James remark, Cathy felt brave enough to say, "Don't they have room service at this hotel?" "Of course," James answered. "Then what are we waiting for James, let's go,"

The ride up in the elevator to James' room was nothing like the last time. The ride up at the Hancock center had been one of spontaneous passion kindled by sparks long suppressed. They were giddy with the joy of finding each other and were like un-caged animals. It was different now, Cathy still had a yearning inside her for James, and she was sure he felt the same, but the weight of incarceration pushing down on them seemed to squeeze out spontaneity and passion, leaving love and compassion. She was sure James had similar feelings. James opened the door to his room and they went inside. There was no mad clutching and kissing like before, James stood by the window and said "Excuse the mess, Cathy, I wasn't expecting company."

"James, I know how difficult this is for you and I feel your pain, why don't we order up dinner and talk about it," Cathy said. She perused the hotel menu, "Would you like to split an order of Crab Alfredo?" "That would be fine," James said, "Order a pot of coffee and something sweet for desert." "You got it," Cathy said and called in the order.

She turned her attention back to James, "I wish there was something I could do, would it help for you to talk to me about it? I promise to keep anything you tell me confidential, James, I just thought it might help if you could talk to someone." Cathy didn't want to pry, but she wished he would open up to her. "How much do you know about your attorney, James, would you like me to check on what kind of success he has had with criminal cases? "You could do that Cathy but it's too late to change now so you might as well save the effort," James said.

"I know you're right, it was something I thought I could do, I feel so useless at this point."

A knock on the door was the welcome news that dinner had arrived. "I'm really not that hungry," Cathy said as she picked at her food. "I'm not either," James said, but they managed to eat most of their dinner.

"I should be heading home, James, I'll be back at court in the morning," she said. "Cathy," James paused, not knowing exactly how to say it, "What would you think of bringing your things with you tomorrow and staying here with me until the trial is over?" "I would love to, James," Cathy said and went to the door. James came over to her and put his arms around her. She held onto him. They stood at the door, not saying anything, holding each other, gathering strength from their union. "Good night James," "Good night Cathy,"

Jury selection was completed the following day and the trial was set to begin with the opening arguments the next day. On their way out of the court house Cathy said, "James, what about a Pizza for dinner tonight?" She didn't feel like a fancy dinner and they couldn't have room service every night. "Sounds good," James said.

After dinner they went to the hotel and watched a movie on TV while lying on the bed. With the movie ended, Cathy went into the bathroom and prepared for bed. She usually slept in the nude, but she slipped on a flimsy nightgown and crawled back up on the bed with James. "Whoa," James said, "You look fantastic." "Good enough to make you forget about tomorrow for a few minutes?" she asked. "Maybe more than that," he said and gave her a quick kiss and went into the bathroom.

Cathy turned down the covers on the bed and climbed inside. James returned from the bathroom in his boxer shorts, turned off the lights and crawled into bed beside her. She slid over so their bodies were in contact from head to toe. They each lay on their side, arms enclosing them. James had one hand in the middle of her back and the other clutched her buttock, pulling her to him. She ran her hand down his back inside his shorts and held him tight. They held each other, moving their hands only slightly and keeping their bodies in close contact. His tensions were ebbing away into the softness of her body. He was enraptured with her responsiveness to his movements. Her breasts pressed against his chest and her hand slid around his hips. She moved away from him just enough to allow her other hand to slip down and caress him under his shorts. She felt the size and hardness of him.

"Cathy, I want you," he said and pulled the covers back and stood up and pulled down his shorts. "Oh my God, you are beautiful," Cathy said as she saw him standing by the bed in the semi-darkness, his trim body culminating in his eager wand projecting upward in front of him. She rolled up and sat on the edge of the bed and put her arms around him as she pressed her face against his stomach. She moved his wand back and forth with the side of her head as she brought her hands to the front and cradled him between them. She slipped her tongue around the head as she fondled his sack. James put his hands on the back of her head and gently pulled her toward him. She let him into her until she started to gag. James held onto her head as he savored the moment. He didn't try to force himself further into her. He held her head steady and enjoyed the rapture of what he was feeling.

He put his hands under her arms and lifted her back onto the bed. She pulled her nightgown over her head and laid on her back, ready for him. She held out her arms and said,

"Come to me, James," He climbed on her and she could feel his wand between her thighs. He cupped her breasts in his hands and kissed her nipples. Cathy was consumed with desire for him, "I want you, James, please!" He guided it in slowly, putting it in and then pulling it out, each time going a little deeper inside her. She didn't know if she could take all of him. But she wanted to try.

She wanted to give him more pleasure than he had ever known. She wanted him to want her more than he had ever wanted a woman. She thrust against him until she could feel him into her completely. She knew now she could take all of him. She thrust herself tightly against him and held on tightly, not moving, concentrating on the feeling of her insides grasping his wand, convulsing around it, amplifying the pleasure for him and for her. The size of him made her convulsions stronger and stronger until she could stand it no longer. "Yes, yes, yes, James," she screamed as her orgasm roared through her. James thrust against her once more, then once more, more forcibly than the last and let out a cry, "Aargdhhhhhhh" as he collapsed on top of her. They lay together, unmoving until James rolled off onto his back. "James, was that your jungle call?" Cathy asked. "Sorry Cathy, do you think anyone heard me?" He said. "Who cares," she replied. She was fulfilled, relaxed and serene for the first time in months.

Chapter Nineteen:

This is the first day of the rest of my life, James thought as they arrived at the courthouse for the opening arguments in his trial. Last night with Cathy had given him a temporary reprieve from the constant pressure he felt over the impending trial. They met Sherman in the hallway as they approached the courtroom. "I'll go on in James so you can talk to Sherman," Cathy said. Sherman prepped James on what to expect during the court session. "We each make opening statements; the prosecutors will present their case to the Judge and jurors and we will then present our case. The judge may recess 'til tomorrow or he may proceed directly to the presentation of evidence."

James and Sherman entered the courtroom and sat at the table for defendants. James looked around for Cathy and saw her sitting about three rows back in the spectator's benches in the gallery. He was surprised to see Ann and Brent's brother seated in the row ahead of Cathy. James had expected a media swarm but was surprised at the furor his case had caused. The courtroom was full, and he had been greeted by bands of demonstrators when he arrived at the courthouse. Some were carrying banners "Thou shalt not kill," Matthew, 5:21 emblazoned on them.

"All rise; Hear Ye, Hear Ye, the Superior Court of the City of San Francisco is now in session. The Honorable Judge Ernst Wilson presiding," the bailiff announced as Judge Wilson entered and took his seat at the bench. "Please be seated and come to order."

Judge Wilson addressed the jury, "Good morning, jurors, you are here to render a verdict in the case of the State of California versus Dr. James Barnett. Dr. Barnett is charged with committing a felony in violation of California Penal Code 401 in the death of Dr. Brent Alswerp, director of Neurology at University Hospital, San Francisco. You will hear opening arguments by the attorneys, the presentation of evidence and closing arguments. You must consider the evidence you hear without prior prejudice clouding your thinking. You are here to impart justice based on the law and only the law. You must isolate yourselves from what you see and hear outside of this courtroom. I will endeavor to assist you with questions of interpretation of how California Law applies to this case as we progress." Judge Wilson then turned to the prosecutors, "You may proceed with your opening arguments."

"Good morning Jurors, I am Richard Meyers, District Attorney for the Northern District of the State of California. We are here this morning to provide the states' evidence against Dr. James Barnett in the death of Dr. Brent Alswerp. California Penal Code 401 states; "Every person who deliberately aids, or advises, or encourages another to commit suicide, is guilty of a felony." We will provide evidence in this case that will convince you, beyond any reasonable doubt, that Dr. Barnett is guilty. We will produce witnesses to this crime and sworn statements made by Dr. Barnett himself that will establish his guilt. Thank you."

Judge Wilson turned to the defense, "You may proceed."

Good Morning Jurors, I am Sherman Burck, attorney for the defendant. We concede to the prosecution that they possess incriminating evidence against my client, Dr. James Barnett, but after you have heard all of the testimony in this case, you will conclude that Dr. Barnett did not, in fact, violate California Penal Code 401. Thank you."

"Is that it?" Cathy thought, that's all he has to say? There must be something he could have said to cast doubt on the case against James.

Judge Wilson addressed the D.A., "You may present your evidence."

"The state calls Dr. Andrew Nerneau." Dr. Nerneau took the stand and was sworn in. "Please state your name and profession;" "Dr. Andrew Nerneau, Certified Anesthesiologist at University Hospital."

"Were you in the operating room when Dr. Barnett performed surgery on Dr. Brent Alswerp?"

"Yes I was; I was the attending anesthesiologist."

"Please describe what you saw."

"When Dr. Alswerp's vitals indicated he was ready for the operation, I told Dr. Barnett he could proceed."

"And what did Dr. Barnett do then?"

"He opened the patients' skull and removed the right frontal parietal lobe, which was placed into a hyperactive antifreeze protein solution."

"At what point in the operation did you declare Dr. Alswerp as clinically dead?"

"When Dr. Barnett removed the right frontal parietal lobe."

"Thank you doctor, your witness, the D.A. said to Sherman."

"Permission to approach the witness," Sherman asked.

"Granted," replied the Judge.

"Did you try, at any time, to stop Dr. Barnett or ask him what he was doing?"

"No, I did not."

"Why was that, this certainly was not a normal procedure, but you did not question Dr. Barnett?"

"Dr. Alswerp had asked us, pleaded with us actually, to perform this procedure."

"Objection on the basis of hearsay Your Honor," the D.A. said.

"Objection sustained," replied the Judge.

Sherman continued, "You say "us," who exactly is "us?"

Dr. Nerneau replied, "Dr. Barnett, myself and Margaret."

"By Margaret, you are referring to Ms. Margaret White, RN, who is also a witness in this trial?"

"Yes."

"Can you tell us why Dr. Alswerp pleaded with you to perform this procedure?"

"Objection, Your Honor," the D.A. said, "Dr. Alswerp's reason for submitting to the operation has no bearing on the law."

"I will allow the question in the interest of understanding the motivations in this case, objection overruled." Judge Wilson responded.

"Please continue, Dr. Nerneau," Sherman said.

"Dr. Alswerp was dying from a rapidly progressing disease known as CJD. He believed he had identified the area in the brain that contained the secret of "Who we are," and had developed a method of extracting and transplanting that section of the brain."

"And you believed him?" Sherman asked.

"Yes."

“Objection, the witness testimony is hearsay,” the D.A. said.

“Objection sustained,” Judge Wilson said. Sherman returned to the defendants table.

“Does the prosecution wish to redirect?” the Judge asked.

“No, Your Honor.”

”You may step down,” Judge Wilson said to Dr. Nerneau.

“The state calls Ms. Margaret White, RN.”

“Please state your name and profession.”

“Margaret White, Registered Nurse at University Hospital.”

“What were your duties at the hospital?”

“I was Dr. Alswerp’s assistant in the operating room.”

“How long did you work under Dr. Alswerp?”

“Six years.”

“And were you present in the operating room on the day of Dr. Alswerp’s operation?”

“Yes, I was.”

“Can you describe what you saw?”

“Dr. Barnett removed a section of Dr.Alswerp’s brain and placed it in a containment Vessel.

“Was Dr. Alswerp alive when Dr. Barnett began the operation?”

“Yes.”

“Was Dr. Alswerp alive when Dr. Barnett finished his operation?”

“No.”

“Thank you Ms. White, your witness.”

Sherman began his questions, “You refer to a vessel; will you describe for me what this vessel contained?”

“Objection, Your Honor, this is hardly germane to the case.”

“The witness has already testified to the existence of the vessel, overruled.” “Please continue, Ms. White,” Judge Wilson ruled.

“What did the vessel contain?”

“It held a solution that Dr. Alswerp had obtained from the Queens University Biological Station in London. I had to arrange with them to obtain it because it was experimental and I recall how odd I thought it was that it was based on the anti-freeze protein from the Arctic Snow Flea.”

“And why this particular fluid used?”Sherman asked.

"It greatly prolongs the integrity of the tissue.”

"Do you know what happened to Dr. Alswerp's body?"

"It was cremated."

"Thank you Ms. White, no further questions."

"The state calls Dr. Alfred Steiner, M.D., PhD."

"Please state your name and profession."

"Dr. Alfred Steiner, medical doctor, doctor of philosophy in Neuroscience, member of the American Neuroscience Association and Director of the Society for Neurological Understanding."

"Thank you Dr. Steiner, in your opinion, is there any way that a patient's frontal parietal lobe could be removed without causing the death of the patient?"

"Absolutely not, I should think the answer to that would be obvious to anyone."

"Perhaps so but we did not want to leave the slightest doubt in the minds of the jury," said the D.A.

"The clerk will strike the statement by the District Attorney from the record," Judge Wilson said.

"The prosecution rests, Your Honor."

"Attorney for the defense, you may call your first witness."

"I call Dr. James Barnett."

"Please state your name and profession,"

"Dr. James Barnett, M.D., neurosurgeon at Trinity Hospital in Chicago, Illinois."

"Dr. Barnett, you studied under Dr. Alswerp and considered him a personal friend is that correct?"

"Yes, Brent was actually my mentor in Med School and for my research residency after graduation."

"And you were personal friends as well?"

"Yes, I frequently sailed with Brent and his wife on their yacht "Adagio."

"So how is it you decided to help him take his own life?"

"Objection, Your Honor, there is no evidence that Dr. Alswerp was a participant."

"Objection sustained."

"Dr. Barnett, how is it you decided to perform an operation on Dr. Alswerp that would surely result in his death?"

"Objection requires a conclusion by the witness."

"Objection sustained."

"Dr. Barnett, how is it you decided to operate on Dr. Alswerp?" Sherman asked.

"Brent's' body was being attacked by CJD, a rare and deadly disease that destroys the brain. He was in the early but unmistakable stage of the disease. He convinced me that his research had identified the location of the center of the 'sense of self' in the brain. The location of "who we are" if you will."

"What made you think you could perform such an operation?" Sherman said.

"Dr. Alswerp had devised a method using the computer aided image navigation system to identify trajectories that could surgically separate the frontal parietal lobe, wherein the "sense of self" resides, from the rest of the brain without destroying the surrounding tissue. The lobe could then be transplanted into a compatible subject at a future time."

"Dr. Barnett, you are an accomplished Neurosurgeon with years of experience, did you think this really was possible?"

"I was skeptical at first, but when Brent showed me the procedure he had devised using the computer aided trajectories, I thought it just might work. Brent pleaded with me to give him a chance to continue his work, to give him a second chance at life."

"Objection, Hearsay, Your Honor."

"Objection sustained."

"So Dr. Barnett, rather than assisting Dr. Alswerp in his suicide, you were assisting him to find a new life"

"Exactly."

"Thank you Dr. Barnett, no further questions."

Judge Wilson asked "Does the prosecution wish to redirect?"

"Yes I do, Your Honor."

"Dr. Barnett, you are asking this jury, a jury of your peers, to accept your story that you did not kill Dr. Alswerp, but gave him a new life?"

"Yes."

"Objection, that's an improper question Your Honor."

"Objection sustained."

"Let me ask you doctor, what actually did happen to Dr. Alswerp's brain that you placed in the vessel?" Is Dr. Alswerp still floating around in that jar, like a gold fish?"

The courtroom broke into laughter, "Order, order in the court," the Judge said, "if there are further outbursts I will ask the bailiff to clear the courtroom."

James did not appreciate the D.A.'s joke. "No sir, he is not."

"Well then, where is he?" the D.A. put his arms up in the air and turned around as if searching the skies for a sign of Dr. Alswerp. His antics brought more laughter from the gallery.

"Order," the Judge said again.

"I will ask you once again, Dr. Barnett, what happened to that piece of Dr. Alswerp's brain that was placed in the vessel?"

Cathy was furious with the prosecutor for the way he was attacking James, and she could see that James was upset, but he controlled his anger.

"It was transplanted into the brain of a suitable subject." James answered. The gallery was buzzing from this latest revelation. "How could that be?" and "Did you hear what he said?" could be overheard.

"Order in the court," Judge Wilson admonished the gallery.

"A suitable subject Dr. Barnett?" the D.A. continued, "what exactly is a suitable subject, and where is that subject now?"

"A suitable subject has physical and clinical characteristics which are compatible with those of the donor." James replied.

"Please answer the second part of my question, Dr. Barnett, "is that suitable subject, as you call him, still alive?"

"Yes he is," James answered.

"Very well," said the D.A. "Please identify this subject for us."

"I am not at liberty to do that," James replied.

"Dr. Barnett, you seem like an intelligent fellow, can you really expect the State of California and the jury in this trial to acquit you of the charge of assisted suicide with a story that you are making up as you go along?"

"Objection, that's an improper question Your Honor."

"Objection sustained."

"No further questions," the D.A. said, "I rest my case."

"Court will be adjourned until tomorrow morning when closing arguments will be heard," the judge said and gaveled the session to an end.

Chapter Twenty:

Cathy waited for James to come out. The hallway was filled with reporters, each one trying to force their microphone in his face for a comment. The trial had created immediate media frenzy. The assisted suicide story had been blasted out of the water by brain transplant hysteria.

A network news reporter thrust his microphone in James face, "Dr. Barnett, will you tell us where your transplant patient is now? Is he still in the hospital? Can he walk? Talk? What can you tell us? "

"No comment"

Another reporter shoved his microphone at James, "Does this person really exist, doctor, or is he a figment of your imagination?"

"No comment"

"Dr. Frankenstein, where is Igor?" someone shouted at him. "Who is this mystery man, Dr. Barnett?" a network reporter asked.

"No Comment" James replied and kept repeating "No comment" to the barrage of questions.

James spotted Cathy and grabbed her arm, "Let's get out of here," he said and they pushed their way through the reporters to the outside. Once outside, they were greeted by a banner that read, "Dr. Barnett's Hypocritical Oath: "I will do harm." They managed to work their way toward Cathy's car and climbed inside. "Let's get a drink." James said. "Amen" Cathy replied. They drove to the hotel and found a quiet booth in the bar to enjoy some peace, away from the crowds.

"It's ironic," Cathy said, "Here I am in the middle of the biggest story of my career, and I can't write a word of it."

"I know, I'm sorry, Cathy, I wish things were different."

"James, I'm worried, watching the testimony today, it looks like a slam dunk for the prosecution."

"I know," he said, but nothing more.

Cathy put her arm around him, moving up close to him. "I love you," she said. If he doesn't want to talk about it, I'm not going to push him, she thought. They finished their drinks and went up to the room.

"Would you like to split an order of Crab Alfredo like we did the other night? Cathy asked.

"That sounds perfect, don't forget to order some coffee and desert to go with it," James responded.

Cathy ordered their dinner from room service and they finished eating just as the network news came on.

"You made the national news, James."

"Tonight's top story," The commentator began, "The defense dropped a bombshell in the murder trial of Dr. James Barnett of Chicago. He is facing second degree murder charges in the assisted suicide case of world renowned neurosurgeon Dr. Brent Alswerp. In testimony today, Dr. Barnett claimed to have transplanted a portion of Dr. Alswerp's brain into the brain of another man. He claims this was done at the request of Dr. Alswerp who was suffering from a rare and debilitating disease. According to Dr. Barnett, his friend, Dr. Brent Alswerp, had located the precise location in our brain that defines "Who we are", and had developed a procedure for transplanting this portion of the brain."

Dr. Barnett insists that Dr. Alswerp pleaded with him to perform the operation in order to save his life so he could continue his research into neurological transfer techniques. Dr. Barnett has refused our request for an interview. We have video of our reporter asking Dr. Barnett to identify the recipient of Dr. Alswerp's brain. "Who is this mystery man, Dr. Barnett?"

"No comment"

"You know Cathy," James said, "I used to think that people that are hounded by the media went out of their way to encourage them. I can see now that they need no encouragement." "I just can't believe how rude some of them can be."

"I know James," Cathy said, "I have always tried to respect the privacy of those I interview but some of my cohorts can be pretty pushy."

The commentator continued, "Skeptics and critics of today's revelations are many, but we have been unable to locate anyone who would go on record to substantiate Dr. Barnett's claims. We asked our medical director, Dr. Anton Werth, to give us his comments. "Would you tell us your opinion of the testimony of Dr. Barnett at today's court hearing, Dr. Werth?"

"Utter nonsense, I'm afraid, it strikes me as a desperate attempt by Dr. Barnett to escape prison for his actions."

"You dumb bastard," James said, he was intrigued by the interview but was getting upset with the pomposity.

"Don't let it upset you James," Cathy gave him a squeeze to let him know she supported him.

"Why do you say that doctor?" The commentator asked.

"The operation that Dr. Barnett describes is science fiction. There has never been a transplant of any part of the human brain. A neurosurgeon will tell you that a transplant of the right frontal lobe is impossible to perform successfully with today's level of expertise."

As a matter of fact, Dr. Werth, we do have a neurosurgeon who is willing to give us his opinion on today's developments, he is Dr. Matthew Getsomi , head of the neurological department at Mercy Hospital here in New York." "Welcome to our show Dr. Getsomi."

"Glad to be with you," he replied. "Did you read the transcript of today's testimony in the trial of Dr. Barnett?" "Yes I did," he responded. "Would you share your comments with us doctor."

James perked up, "This guy is no idiot," he said, "I know some of his work and it is pretty good. I wonder what he will have to say."

"First of all," Dr. Getsomi said, "Let me say that I have read most of the published works of Dr. Alswerp and found them to be on the cutting edge of where we are in our current understanding of the human brain. He did not publish anything relative to his recent work and I therefore cannot express an opinion on that body of work. I do not know Dr. Barnett personally, but I know he is very highly regarded and at the forefront of new techniques in cranial surgery."

"So far so good," James said, "but I feel a "but" coming on.

"Insofar as the claims made in court today," Dr. Getsomi continued, "I am afraid they stretch credibility and border on the preposterous." "Our operating techniques on the human brain have not developed to the extent where an operation such as Dr. Barnett describes could be considered even remotely possible."

"James', Cathy said, "I hate to say it, but until now I didn't really appreciate the enormous breakthrough you achieved. Your name is going to be in the history books for great medical accomplishments."

"Let's hope it's not as a convicted felon." He responded.

"So in your opinion, Dr. Getsomi, the scenario that Dr. Barnett described in court today is not to be believed?"

"I think you would have to say that at best it would be extremely unlikely and I for one would be absolutely astounded if it were true."

"I can't argue with anything he said," James remarked, "If I were in his shoes, I would probably express the exact same opinions."

"You are too magnanimous, James," Cathy said as she scrunched up closer to him.

"Thank you for your comments, Dr. Getsomi, and now turning to other news of the day." The TV anchor continued.

"Let's see if we can find a movie to watch," James said.

"Great idea," Cathy snuggled up to him and put her arm over his chest as they lay on the bed pretending to watch the movie. Cathy knew that if they found James guilty tomorrow, as things now appeared, she might never again have the chance to be with him as she was now. She drifted off to sleep and when she awoke it was daylight. She was still in her clothes from last night. Great, she thought, what could be my last night with him and I fall asleep in my clothes. James was not in bed and Cathy was afraid he may have gotten up and left already. Her fears were quieted when she heard the shower in the bathroom. Thank God, she thought.

She disrobed and opened the shower door a crack, "Is there room in there for two?" she said.

"C'mon in here, you," James said and helped her into the shower. The soapy water was running down his body and off his protruding parts. He moved over so Cathy could get wet and rubbed her back with the soap. He ran his soapy hands over her shoulders and her breasts. The warm, soapy water swished between them as he pulled her up against him.

She lost herself in the sensuous heat of the shower, her body slip, sliding against him. She felt his wand growing stronger as she squirmed in his arms, his hands rubbing up and down her soapy body which was responding rapturously.

She turned around and faced him so her breasts were against him with her arms encircling his back. The warm soapy water was washing over them. James grabbed her buttocks with both hands and lifted her up 'til his face was buried in her breasts. She wrapped her legs around him and held on as he raised her up and then let her down until she felt his hardened tool entering into her. She squirmed against him to help it into the right spot. He moved her up and down with his hands as he went deeper into her. She held onto his shoulders and dropped her body down onto him until he was completely buried inside her.

She held on and squirmed with pleasure. Her insides began convulsing, grabbing onto him and releasing him as their emotions reached a crescendo. James held on tight as they forced their bodies together. Cathy's' last vestige of control abandoned her as they screamed in unison. James did his jungle cry as her orgasm overtook her. She clutched his body with her arms and tightened her legs around him. When Cathy stopped clenching, James set her down and they finished their shower.

James said "Here Cathy," and handed her a towel as they stepped outside the shower. He took the other towel and began drying her off.

"A Ha," Cathy thought, that's why he gave me the towel. She returned the favor and rubbed him with her towel. She couldn't resist spending a little extra time on his private parts.

"That was fun," Cathy said as they finished and started dressing for their trip to the court.

James ecstasy slowly eroded as he felt the heaviness return to his heart.

On the drive to the courthouse, Cathy said, “You know, James, I’m thinking this fellow Chase Hartley that I’ve been tracking for a story has to be your mystery man. I know that you operated on him the day after Dr. Alswerp.”

“I can’t help you with that,” was all James would say.

“I knew you wouldn’t,” Cathy said.

Chapter Twenty One:

When they reached the courthouse, the crowds were overflowing onto the street. The TV coverage had made its impact. They continued on and parked in back of the courthouse and came in from the opposite side of the crowds. They were almost in the building before someone spotted them and began shouting insults. They were early and there were only a few people in the hallway.

James pulled on her arm, “C'mon Cathy, there's someone I want you to meet.” They approached a middle aged man and an attractive woman standing by the entrance to the courtroom.

“Ann, Henry, I would like you to meet my friend, Cathy.” Under the circumstances, Cathy thought “friend” was about all she could hope for.

“How nice to meet you,” Ann said, looking at James with a look Cathy found hard to describe. Henry was polite, but definitely not friendly.

Ann took James hand in hers and said, “Good luck today, Jimmy.” Cathy could tell that she really meant it.

“Yes, James, good luck,” Henry said, but Cathy wasn't sure he meant it. The obvious attachment between Ann and James made her wonder if Ann was one of James' former lovers.

Before she could ask him, he said, "Ann is Brent Alswerp's widow, we have been good friends for years." "And Henry?" Cathy asked.

"Brent's brother."

"Oh, he's the one who sued you?"

"Right," James replied.

They were standing in the aisle at the back of the gallery when James said, "I have to go up front now Cathy." She held onto his hand tightly as he looked her in the eyes and said, "I'll see you later."

She put her arm around him and held him close, wondering if she would ever again feel the thrill of his body touching hers. "I love you James," she whispered.

"I love you too, he whispered in her ear," and left for the defense table. The jurors filed into the jury box, and the District Attorney's staff took their seats. Sherman leaned over close to James and said "We are in a lot of trouble here James, if you have anything you can give me to help us out here, now is the time."

"I'm sorry Sherman, but I can't tell you anything more."

"All rise. Hear Ye, Hear Ye, the Superior Court of the City of San Francisco is now in session. The Honorable Judge Ernst Wilson presiding," the bailiff announced as Judge Wilson entered and took his seat at the bench. “Please be seated and come to order.”

“The prosecution may proceed with their closing argument,” Judge Wilson said.

“Thank you, Your Honor. Ladies and gentlemen of the jury, I would like to begin by reading to you the California Penal Code 401: *Every person who deliberately aids, or advises, or encourages another to commit suicide, is guilty of a felony.* The state has presented irrefutable evidence provided by those present at the time of Dr. Brent Alswerp’s death that the defendant, Dr. James Barnett, did knowingly and deliberately perform an operation on Dr. Alswerp that resulted in his death. This was not the sympathetic act of a doctor providing medicine to a dying patient to self-administer. This was the overt act of a doctor with a scalpel in his hand, to knowingly put an end to life. Putting aside the moral depravity of the act, the total disregard for another human being’s life demands that Dr. Barnett be convicted of this crime and receive the maximum sentence permissible under the statue. Ladies and gentlemen of the jury, Dr. Barnett does not deny performing the act, the law is clear and he must be punished for his crime. The evidence leaves no other possible conclusion. He is guilty of second degree murder for taking the life of Dr. Brent Alswerp.” The D.A. returned to the prosecutors table exuding an air of victory, if ever he felt he had an open and shut case, it was this one.

“The defense may present their closing argument,” the Judge directed.

“Thank you, Your Honor. Ladies and gentlemen of the jury,” Sherman began, “This was not the cold blooded murder that the prosecution wants you to believe, this is the compassionate act of a man who idolized his friend and mentor. Dr. Barnett studied under Dr. Alswerp for over two years and the two became close friends. When Dr. Alswerp contracted the deadly CJD, he pleaded with his good friend, Dr. Barnett to give him a chance for life, not death. Dr. Alswerps’ ground breaking research in brain function has been heralded in the scientific community. His insight into the intricacies of neural connections gave him the opportunity to devise a means of separating the portion of the brain that determines “who we are.” Dr. Alswerp convinced his friend of the efficacy of an operation to remove the “who we are” portion of his brain to be stored and later transplanted in a suitable donor in order that he could continue his important life’s work. I propose to you, ladies and gentlemen of the jury, that Dr. Barnett is not the cruel murderer the state would have you believe, but a caring and devoted physician endeavoring to provide a good friend with an alternative to death.” Sherman returned to the table for the defense and put his hand on James shoulder in support. It did not look good for James.

“Does the prosecution seek rebuttal?” Judge Wilson asked.

“Yes,” Your Honor, the D.A. said as he rose from the table to address the jury. “The defense would like you to believe that this was an act of compassion. A doctor performing a life saving operation on a friend to offer him a chance for a new life. Do I really have to tell you how preposterous this is? Do we really believe that Dr. Brent Alswerp is floating around in a jar, or implanted in someone’s head?” The D.A. was definitely enjoying himself as he pranced to and fro in front of the jury box, his confidence building with the rise in his voice. “If we are to believe such nonsense, where is Dr. Alwerp?” He raised his arms into the air and looked up as if he was searching the heavens. “Where is he?” He pranced back and forth; he looked behind the bench he looked under the tables. Laughter erupted in the courtroom. The D.A. continued, “If he’s not in the jar, he said derisively, where is he?”

“I can answer that question,” A strong voice from the gallery interrupted the D.A.’s speech. It was Chase Hartley, Cathy recognized him from ‘photos as he stood up. The courtroom erupted in turmoil as the Judge pounded his gavel to bring order.

“Order, Order in the court,” he shouted, but the chaos continued. “Bailiffs remove that man from the courtroom,” he said. Court will recess for one hour.” Judge Wilson motioned for the prosecutors and the defendants’ lawyer to follow him to his chambers.

"James, will you catch up with that man and keep him in the hallway until I get there? I have to meet with the Judge but I'll be with you as soon as I can." Sherman said as he headed for the Judges chamber.

James rushed out to the hallway. "Chase hold up, my attorney Sherman Burck, wants to talk to you. I'm sure he wants to know if you will testify if he can get the Judge's approval."

"Of course I will; that's why I came. I've been following your case and I could see you were going to be convicted if I didn't show up."

Cathy sat stunned in her seat. "I knew it," she thought,"I knew it." It should have been so obvious, the timing of the operations and the incredible academic performance of Chase after the procedure. Chase Hartley was Brent Alswerp; or Brent Alswerp was Chase Hartley. She couldn't wrap her mind around it. She wished James had told her the whole story. She hoped Chase would be able to help James' case, and wondered why he had waited so long. Her thoughts were going in circles as she tried to tie everything together.

Sherman entered the Judges' chambers and asked if he could be excused for a few minutes to learn the identity of the man who had caused the scene and if he had a bearing on the case. Judge Wilson granted his request and Sherman caught up with James and Chase. “James told me you are Dr. Chase Hartley, is that correct?” Sherman asked.

“Yes it is,” Chase answered.

“Let me make a wild guess; are you the recipient of Dr. Alswerp's frontal lobe?”

“That would be correct,” Chase replied.

“I’ve got to get back to the Judges’ chambers. Stay here, I’ll be back when I find out if they will agree to let you testify,” Sherman said as he hurried away.

“What did you learn counselor?” Judge Wilson asked when Sherman returned.

“The man who caused the disturbance claims to be Dr. Chase Hartley the recipient of the right frontal parietal lobe of Dr. Brent Alswerp's brain.”

“I see,” the judge said with a deepening frown.

“I realize it is unheard of to take testimony after closing arguments have begun Your Honor but this man could be a pivotal witness in this case and I believe his testimony is crucial to obtaining a just verdict for the defendant.”

“What is your stance in this matter Mr. Meyers?” Judge Wilson asked the D.A.

“Since we have no information on this person through the discovery process, I would be inclined to resist any attempt to allow his testimony in court. I realize this would open the door for a long appeal process which would prove expensive for the state but on the other hand a mistrial would be equally costly. If you decide to continue with the trial Your Honor, we would abide by your decision."

"I will consider this matter and let you know my decision when court resumes," Judge Wilson stated.

"All rise. Hear Ye, Hear Ye, the Superior Court of the City of San Francisco is now in session. The Honorable Judge Ernst Wilson presiding," the bailiff announced as Judge Wilson entered and took his seat at the bench. "Please be seated and come to order."

"Ladies and gentlemen of the jury," the Judge began, "The disruption to this trial would normally require me to declare a mistrial, but after a conference in my chambers, the prosecution and the defense have agreed to hear testimony from a new defense witness. With the best interests of the State of California in mind, I have decided to allow this trial to proceed.

Sherman grasped James arm to signify his pleasure with the Judges' decision.

"The defense calls Dr. Chase Hartley to the stand," Sherman said. Chase took the oath and sat in the witness box.

"Please state your name and profession,"

"Dr. Chase Hartley, also known as Dr. Brent Alswerp," Chase replied, his answer creating an uproar in the gallery.

Ann grabbed Henry's arm as she felt the blood drain from her head. She had wondered what Chase was up to when he interrupted the D.A. but she never imagined it would be this. Her head was spinning with the words she had just heard, this can't be real, she thought, it must be a dream. The man she knew as Chase was actually Brent? Her mind could not grasp the implications of what was unfolding before her. She thought of her display of lust on Adagio. She had never made love to Brent with such abandonment as she had to the man she knew as Chase. What must he think of her and who is he, Chase or Brent, her mind couldn't comprehend it.

"Order, order in the court," the Judge said, rapping his gavel, "If there are any more outbursts, I will have the courtroom cleared."

Sherman continued his questioning, "Please tell the court why you say your name is Dr. Brent Alswerp when we all know that Dr. Alswerp is dead." I am not dead, but very much alive," he said.

"How is it that you can make that statement doctor?" Sherman asked.

"The operation that Dr. Barnett performed was an outstanding success, it not only gave me a new life, a chance to continue my work, but it also allowed Chase

Hartley, as I am now known, to live a normal life instead of being confined to life support for the rest of his days."

"Thank you, doctor, your witness," Sherman said to the D.A. as he returned to the table for the defense with a bounce he had been lacking throughout the trial.

The D.A. began, "Dr. Hartley, you have testified that you are also known as Dr. Brent Alswerp, is that correct?"

"I am not known as Dr. Brent Alswerp, I am known as Dr. Chase Hartley, but I am Dr. Brent Alswerp," Chase answered.

"That being the case, do you have Dr. Alswerp's social security number?"

"No"

"Do you have a Drivers License that identifies you as Dr. Brent Alswerp?"

"No"

"Then what do you have of Dr. Alswerp?"

"His identity, which determines "who we are, for instance, I can see my brother Henry in the gallery; remember the time we stole the licorice from the candy store, Henry?" Henry nodded his head in agreement but he was filled with disbelief as Dr. Hartley was testifying to be Brent.

Chase continued, "I may not have Dr. Alswerp's fingerprints and I may not look like him, but I have his "who we are" and that's what counts, so you see, Dr. Barnett should not be on trial for my murder, because I'm still here."

The D.A. was totally flustered, he went over to the Judge, shaking his head and throwing his hands in the air. The Judge seemed equally nonplussed. "Court is adjourned, we will reconvene in the morning," he said and gaveled the proceedings to an end.

It was bedlam in the gallery. Chase came back to see Ann and she was livid.

"How could you do this to me," she said, "How could you," her voice cracked as she slapped him across the face. Chase reached to hold her arm.

"Don't touch me!" she screamed, and hurried out of the courtroom.

Chase turned to Henry, "I'm sorry I had to put you all through this," he said. Henry looked at him quizzically. He didn't quite understand what was happening. "I'm sorry, Henry," Chase said again and turned to James who had come to see Cathy.

"Chase, I would like you to meet my friend, Cathy." There it was again, "his friend."

"Very nice to meet you Cathy," Chase said. She was sure he didn't remember her name from her attempt to see him at

NSCT. "Chase, you must join Cathy and me for dinner, what do you say?"

"I would like that. We have a lot to talk about."

They left the courthouse and were mobbed by reporters wanting comments from James and Chase. "No comment," "No comment," was all they got.

Chapter Twenty Two:

They had dinner at the hotel restaurant where they would not be bothered by the media. Cathy was dying to hear what Chase had to say about what he was doing.

"So James," he started out, "I guess you have been pretty busy lately with all the legal hassle, Janet kept me up to date and lately the media has been all over it." I'm sorry I had you sworn to secrecy, but now you can see why it was necessary. Our lives will never be the same."

"What about you, Chase, what have you been doing?"

"It's kind of a long story James; you remember our talks about the problem of finding recipients for parietal lobe transplants? The ethical considerations are as difficult to solve as the technical and biological problems of the transplant since the recipient loses his or her identity in favor of that of the donor. The difficulties of finding recipients with the required blood type, chromosome match, physical and psychological profile make it unlikely a doctor could find a suitable prospect.

We concluded that human cloning was the only practical solution. For my Doctoral Thesis I worked on the development of an automated cell transfer method that improved survival rate of fertilized eggs to over 97% which makes human cloning much more viable. As you know James, the failure rate had been so horrendous it presented a huge barrier to successful cloning. With a success rate now over 97% the moral and ethical problems of dealing with the rejects becomes manageable. I am confident that we will eventually see success rates approaching 100% which would provide a supply of clones for transplant. You would be amazed at the number of famous people they have as clients at NSCT.

"But you still have the moral problems connected with caring for the rejects and modifying the successful clones." Cathy said.

"You're right Cathy," Chase went on, "The number of rejects early on created a problem for NSCT. I do know that with the higher success rate, fewer clones will be required to insure continuity for any individual."

Cathy's phone was vibrating, she had the sound turned off, but she checked the caller ID and it was from Kingman. "Excuse me, James, Chase, I have to take this call." Cathy went into the lobby and answered her call.

"Ms. Nichols, this is Martin Green, I have the diner on route 93, you said to call you with any news about that clinic."

"Yes, Martin, what is it?"

"Well, a little while ago this young boy, I think he is about 13 years old, came in here scared out of his wits and asked me to protect him. He's from the clinic, Ms. Nichols, so I called you."

My God, Cathy thought, how ironic, having dinner with James and Chase when this happens. "Listen Martin, I am leaving right now to drive down there, don't tell anyone about this, especially the sheriffs' office, I should be there in about 8 hours. Please keep the boy comfortable until I get there.

Cathy returned to the restaurant, "James, I'm sorry, but I have an emergency and I have to leave right away. I won't be able to be in court tomorrow, but you know you will be in my thoughts, I just know you will be acquitted, they don't have any other choice, do they?"

"Bye Chase, it was nice meeting you." Cathy said as she left.

"Cathy wait!" James said as he got up and caught her at the door. "Is there anything I can do to help you?"

"That is so sweet James, in the middle of the trial of your life, you think of me. I'll be all right, I just got a big break in an investigation I have been working on for months and I have to check it out. I will do everything I can to get back before your trial ends," she gave James a hug and a kiss and hurried away.

"So tell me James is Cathy your west coast girl, or is she someone special?" Chase asked as James returned to the table.

"Actually she is someone very special Chase, I think she might be the one." James answered.

"That's great James, I hope it works out for you, but now that we are alone, I want to tell you the really exciting part, listen to this James, as I told you when I called the other day, I have discovered a means of locking onto the propagation frequency of the Alpha brain waves. I can lock on to them and unscramble them just like a modem demodulates a digitized analog signal. You have to come out to my lab and see this James." What this means is that instead of having to physically cut out the lobe and transplant it, I will be able to synchronize the transfer of the content in the lobe to the recipient. You know James, it is kind of like doing "copy and paste" on your computer." Chase was very intent on James understanding the significance of his discovery. "Let's get out of here James, I want you to come down to my lab in Half Moon Bay and see what I'm talking about with your own eyes."

On their way to Half Moon Bay James asked Chase about Ann.

"I saw the exchange with Ann in the courtroom today, if you don't mind my asking, what was that all about?" James queried.

"Well, I don't know if you heard that I bought 'Adagio' from Ann through a broker, but I re-commissioned her and after she was launched I kept the boat at the club dock. Ann came by one day when I was aboard to check on the old girl and I invited her aboard. It was the first time we had 'met' and we got along really well if you know what I mean.

Anyway, I guess when she found out I was not who she thought I was, she felt, understandably so, that she had been lied to and that I had taken advantage of her."

"I see why she was so upset," James said.

"I know James, I tried to tell her the whole story one day but she didn't want hear it. I let my passion get in the way of my reason. Now I know I should have made her listen to me. I still love her James. I hope she will forgive me someday."

Chase approached the security guard when they arrived at NSCT. "Evening George, I brought my friend from Chicago to see my lab, would you let us in?"

"You know I'm not supposed to do it Dr. Hartley but seeing it's you, I guess it will be OK." He opened the door for Chase and James to make their way to the lab.

"Here it is James," Chase said, "This is where I do all of my research." James was impressed with the array of equipment at Chases' disposal.

"I've seen university labs that couldn't compare with this," he said. "Thanks James, but wait until you see this," Chase said as he removed two thumb drives from his pocket.

"You carry those around with you?" James asked.

"I can't take a chance on someone hacking into my computer to get to my data. I dump the data every time I leave the lab. These two thumb drives hold sixty four gigabytes. I never let them out of my possession," Chase said as he inserted the thumb drives into the computer. James watched the monitors as Chase accessed his data. "This is one of my recent experiments James. The subject you see on the monitor has been fitted with electrodes to transmit his brain waves to the computer and the monitor on your right is showing the unscrambled data after it is processed by my program."

James moved closer to the monitor, there was intermittent static on the screen but there were also images of what the subject was thinking. "Oh my God Chase, I can't believe my eyes. Is this what it appears to be? How did you ever work this out? This is earth shattering. I can hardly grasp the significance of this." James put his hands on Chases' shoulders and looked him in the eyes, "You are a genius my friend, how did you ever do it?"

"All I can say James, is that there was a lot of Devine Intervention," Chase answered. James was overwhelmed, all he was able to say was "Incredible."

On the drive back to the hotel, James said "Now I can understand why you carry all your research with you on those thumb drives. There are people who would literally kill to get that data."

"I know." Chase replied, "It frightens me sometimes when I think of how much our Lord has entrusted in me.

“I’m glad you took me to the lab Chase, I never could have fully realized what you were saying until I saw it with my own eyes. To fulfill the mission you have embarked upon, you still need a healthy clone and you still have the moral issue of implanting foreign material into its brain.” James said.

“True, but now, instead of having to wait ten years until the clones brain is large enough for the physical transplant, we can begin electronic transfer as early as three or four and progressively transfer more information until the transfer is complete. The beauty of this is that we aren’t destroying anything in the clone, we are only supplementing their natural learning.” “This is the future James,” Chase was enthusiastic but James was troubled. “I don’t think society is ready for human cloning, Chase, the moral conundrum must be resolved.” James said.

“I believe that problem will dissipate as each successful transfer has occurred,” Chase responded, “NSCT has a facility in Kingman, Arizona where they do the cloning and monitor the development of the clones. They have a complete medical staff to care for defective clones. I have never been down there but I plan to visit next month.”

“Think about it James, we will be able to perpetuate the brilliant minds of the world, scientists like Galileo and Leonardo da Vinci, humanitarians like Abraham Lincoln, Martin Luther King, Helen Keller and Mother Teresa. Just imagine what our world might be like if these great people and others like them had been able to continue their work indefinitely."

"I can't deny the possible benefits of what you describe could very well change the course of human destiny for the better, but I have some serious caveats. First of all, you would have to improve the success rate for cloning to near perfect before society would accept the concept and the rejects would have to be cared for in a humane manner. Secondly, the transfer of "who we are" would have to be accomplished in a gradual and non-invasive manner so as not to disrupt the psyche of the clone. If all this could be done successfully, I think you might have a shot at it. In fact, I might sign up myself some day," James said.

"Well, I couldn't ask for anything more than that James, but all this has my brain worn out, how about a brandy when we get back to the hotel?" Chase asked.

"Great idea," James replied.

They returned to the hotel lounge and ordered Grand Marnier. They sipped their brandy and reminisced of their past friendship. "I really enjoyed this evening, James, it was so nice to see you again," Chase said. "I'll meet you in court tomorrow James. What time do they start?"

"Nine o'clock sharp," James responded.

"OK, see you then."

"Chase, before you go I wanted to say that I too enjoyed our evening. It was a good night.   It's been much too long since we were able to visit like that," James said. As they parted James was still having a lot of trouble reconciling Brent's persona in Chase's body.

Chapter Twenty Three:

Cathy drove through the night, anxious to reach Kingman and learn what the boy could tell her. She had no trouble staying awake, the adrenaline driving her on. It was 5:15 in the morning when she pulled up in front of the Diner. It was dark inside, except for a small night light. She didn't want to disturb Martin or the boy so she decided to wait in the car until daylight. Just then the door to the Diner opened and Martin came out to the car.

"I've been watching for you," he said, "the boy is sleeping inside, I moved a couple of benches together and made up a place for him to sleep."

"Thanks for doing this Martin; do you have any hot coffee inside?" Cathy could feel the adrenaline ebbing away and needed to stay awake until she could talk to the boy."

"C'mon in," Martin said as he went in and turned on a small light. He poured a cup of coffee for Cathy as she sat on a stool at the counter. She saw the boy lying on the benches, there was nothing remarkable about him, she thought, he looked like any other thirteen year old. He was average size, light skinned for an African American, with dark hair. She hoped he would wake up soon.

"What has he told you?" she asked Martin.

"Well," Martin began, "it was slow yesterday evening so I decided to close early and I was cleaning up out back when I saw this boy huddled behind my shed. I asked him what he was doing there and he said, I'm hiding, please don't tell them I'm here." "Who is 'them'," I asked him.

"Up the road," he said, and pointed toward the clinic. "That's when I decided I better call you. I'm afraid of those people and I didn't know what to do, there's been a helicopter with a searchlight flying around most of the night."

Cathy knew she had to notify the authorities, but until she talked to the boy she really wasn't sure who to call. She imagined that local enforcement agencies were likely compromised. "Did you ask his name?"

"Simpson 187," Martin replied. Just then the boy sat up and stretched.

"Good morning, I'm Cathy Nichols and I'm here to help you, I understand you are from the clinic up the road, is that right?" The boy nodded. "How were you able to get out?"

"Me and my two friends, Douglas 93 and McCartney 101, noticed that our 'teacher' would fall asleep in his chair sometimes after dinner and this week they are doing some drain work behind our building and there was a space under the fence they hadn't closed up. We figured we could sneak past our 'teacher' when he dozed off and get out under the fence before they caught us. We didn't know there was an alarm on the door and when we went out it went off and woke up the 'teacher'. He caught Douglas 93 before we even got to the fence, I got under the fence and got away but McCartney 101 got snagged on the wire and they caught up with him."

Oh my, Cathy thought, what this boy has been through. "Why did you want to run away from the clinic?" she asked.

"We didn't want to be next. Some of our friends would be taken away and we never knew what happened to them. Whenever Dr. Heinrich came in to the section and took one of us away, no one would ever see them again. We heard rumors that they were locked up in another building with children from other sections."

"What do you mean other sections?" Cathy said.

"We were moved every few years as we got older, from section one to section two and so on. I was in section six which I think is the last one."

Cathy looked at Martin, "I have heard enough, I'm calling the F.B.I., this is clearly a violation of U.S. Human Rights Laws, and I don't trust the locals." She called Peter, "I need your help, Peter," she said, and explained the situation to him. "I need the F.B.I. here right away, but Peter, please don't send a camera crew, we are not ready for that."

"Martin, I think we should lock up until the F.B.I. arrives, the clinic people may come here looking for him."

"Agents from the Phoenix Office of the F.B.I. will be there in an hour." Peter told her. Cathy was fascinated by Simpson 187.

"How long have you been at the clinic?" She asked.

"I've never been anywhere else,"

"What do you do all day? Describe a typical day for me."

"The alarms go off at 6 AM, we have breakfast at 7, class from 8 to 11, exercise from 11 to 12, lunch from 12 to 1, class from 1 to 4, exercise from 4 to 5, dinner from 5 to 6 and reading from 6 to 9 when we go to bed and they turn off the lights."

"Do you ever see your parents?"

"We don't have parents, we're clones."

Cathy was shocked, she had suspected it, but hearing him say it still made her head spin.

The excited barking of bloodhounds was becoming louder until they were right outside. "Open up, you have something of ours and we want it back," the men shouted as they pounded on the door.

"Don't open the door Martin," Cathy pleaded. Martin looked worried and confused, but did not unlock the door.

"OK, then, we'll be back with the sheriff and you'll go to jail." Cathy prayed the F.B.I. would get there before they returned.

An unmarked car pulled in front of the diner and two men got out and approached the door. Please God, let it be the F.B.I. They knocked on the door.

"F.B.I." one of them said. Cathy sprang to the door and unlocked it. She could have hugged them, she was so happy they had made it before the sheriff came.

"Are you Ms. Nichols?" "Yes and here is Simpson 187, she led them to the boy. "He escaped from the compound down the road, he's very frightened," Cathy said, "please be gentle with him."

"That compound is a human cloning factory" Cathy said, "They were here a half hour ago with bloodhounds demanding we release the boy to them. I'm afraid if you don't act fast, they will destroy evidence and be gone by the time you arrive."

"Let us talk to the boy, Ms." The agent said and they sat down and talked to Simpson 187. It wasn't long before they huddled at the end of the diner talking on their cell phones.

When they returned, one of the agents said, "we were able to obtain a federal search warrant, a task force will be assembling here shortly. The boy will go with us to aid us in the search." Cathy was impressed by their efficiency. She didn't think the government could ever move that swiftly.

Cathy decided it was time to get the camera crew. She called Peter and said "You have to get a 'copter and crew here right away. This is going down within the hour." I'll do what I can," Peter answered.

The sheriff's car pulled up with its siren blaring. The men had returned as threatened. They had no idea who they were dealing with as they approached. The sheriff started in on Martin, "I'm arresting you for –" the two men with him made an effort to grab Simpson 187 "this is our property" one of them said as he was about to push the agent aside.

"F.B.I." the agent said flashing his badge in one hand and a revolver in the other. "Sheriff, arrest these men, strip them of their cell phones and any weapons and hold them in your squad car until we give you further instructions."

"Now wait a minute," the sheriff began, but the body language of the agents convinced him to back off and follow directions.

The Task Force began assembling outside. The helicopters were first, followed by the armored S.W.A.T. truck and a dozen federal enforcement cars. "Ok, let's go, c'mon son, show us where you live," the agents said as they went outside and joined the Task Force. It looked like an army invasion, Cathy thought. The stream of cars and trucks with the helicopters overhead was a fearsome sight as they headed down the road.

“Damn, where are our people, the biggest story of my life and I’m going to miss it,” but then she heard the whir of the helicopter blades as it settled down in front of the diner. “I thought you guys would never get here. Tom, get in my car with your camera.

Follow my car to the compound she shouted to the pilot, the Task Force just left minutes ago. We should still be able to get a shot of them pulling up to the gate.” She jumped in her car and they headed down the road.

In the excitement of the morning Cathy had almost forgotten James was on his way to court. She should tell him now what was going down. She called him on her phone.

“James,” she said.

“Hi Cathy,”

“Good luck this morning, is Chase with you?”

“No, he’s meeting me at the courthouse.”

“I’m sure his testimony will clear you, there’s no way they can convict you of murdering someone who’s not dead. Listen James, this emergency I told you about, I’m afraid it’s going to cause Chase a lot of trouble. I don’t know the extent of his involvement, but the company he works for has a human cloning factory here in Kingman.”

“A what?”

“A human cloning factory, James, they grow clones, I suspect hundreds of them, it will be on our news feed this afternoon. I really hope this doesn’t jeopardize your trial, but I imagine Chase will hear about it this morning. There’s no way I could hold up on this. The F.B.I. is raiding the compound as we speak.”

“Oh Lord.”

“I wanted to give you a little advance warning in case you want to talk to Chase. The call I got last night at dinner was about a clone that had escaped from the compound. I just hope Chase isn’t too deep in this thing. The boy I talked to is 13 years old, so the company was into this a long time before Chase went to work for them. James, please call me and let me know what happens in court, OK?”

“OK Cathy, but listen, I’m really upset about this cloning thing. When Chase was talking about it last night I thought it was hypothetical, I had no idea they were actually doing it.”

“I know, gotta go James, I’ll talk to you later.”

The gate keepers were gone so Cathy drove right into the compound. The F.B.I. was rounding up everyone in the buildings and moving them outside. There were pregnant women who looked like they were due to deliver momentarily. There were children that looked like they ranged in age from two years to 15 years. There were doctors and nurses, it was a chaotic scene. She wanted to be sure the camera crew was getting it all. Cathy approached a pregnant woman, "When are you due to deliver?"

"Next week," the woman answered.

"Do you know who the donor is?"

"No idea," she answered.

"How much were you paid to do this?"

"I'd rather not say," was the reply. "We're called 'hens' the woman said, we have to come in every two months for an ultrasound, and if they don't like what they see, they take the baby."

Cathy drove to the back of the compound. There was a small maintenance building that had machinery inside. At the corner of the property there was a large trash compactor and an incinerator. With such a large trash compactor, Cathy wondered why they also needed an incinerator. She felt her stomach churn as a feeling of foreboding swept over her. "You don't suppose," she thought.

She was interrupted by Tom, her cameraman, "What are we doing back here, Cathy, I don't see anyone to interview."

"Let's check out that incinerator, Tom, I'm really afraid of what we might find there." Tom looked at her and she could tell he shared her fear. Cathy pulled on the large handle that latched the doors but couldn't budge it. Tom took over and yanked it open. They looked at the pile of ash on the bottom of the chamber. Cathy grabbed Tom's arm, she almost hit the concrete as she saw what looked like human bones in the ash. "Oh God, what have they done here?" she could barely get the words out. Tom wasn't much better off. He held onto the frame to steady himself.

"Cathy, I'm sorry, I don't think I can handle this." Tom was still holding onto the metal door frame, staring down at the gruesome scene at the bottom of the incinerator. "Take some footage of this and let's go find an agent to check this out." Cathy said.

They found the agents that were at the diner questioning a nurse.

"What are you doing here?" You're not supposed to be in here, you'll have to leave right now," He told them.

"OK," Cathy said, "but first you have come to the back of the compound and see what we found in the incinerator." He looked at Cathy in a way that indicated his concern at what he might find.

"Let's check it out," he told his partner. They followed Cathy and Tom to the incinerator. "Oh my God," he said as he surveyed the ashes, "call in the forensics people for this," he told his partner. "We have to seal off this area until they arrive." He turned to Cathy, "You have to get out of here now, but hey, I really appreciate your calling this place to our attention. I would never have believed something like this could exist in our country."

They were on their way out of the compound when they saw a commotion at a building next to the Section Five building. Fifteen or twenty F.B.I. agents were crowded into the front doors of the building. Cathy and Tom sidled their way along the edge of the crowd trying to get a glimpse of what was happening. Then she saw a doctor in a white coat holding something that looked like an igniter.

"Get out of my hospital." "Stay back or I will blow up this building and everyone in it." He shouted. She could see tanks of Oxygen or something similar and she assumed he had opened the valves to fill the space with the gas. There were several children in beds in the room as the standoff continued. The children looked to range in age from about five to fifteen years. They were terrified and some of them were huddled together in fear.

"Dr. Heinrich!" an F.B.I. agent hollered at him, "Put down the igniter and come out of the building."

"No, never," the doctor shouted back, and what followed was the most horrific scene Cathy had ever witnessed. Dr. Heinrich ignited the gas and there was an enormous explosion. Broken glass and bricks were flying everywhere. She and Tom were knocked off their feet into a row of hedges in front of the building. She could see several of the agents were injured by flying debris.

There was nothing she could do to rescue the children inside as the building was engulfed in flames. Cathy crawled out on the grass and collapsed, sobbing. She was heartbroken, she thought of those children dying such a painful death. She thought her insides were coming out.

"Are you OK Cathy?" Tom said.

"Yes, I think so, are you all right Tom?" She could see blood running down the side of his face.

"I'm alright Cathy, just a scrape on my forehead."

"Let's get out of here," she said as Tom helped her regain her feet. Cathy saw an F.B.I. agent coming toward them. "We can't let them confiscate our cameras," she said as they hurried to reach Cathy's car.

She thought of James. Today should be the final day of the trial and she was anxious to get back to the city so she could be with him when the jury brought in their verdict.

"Tom, would you drive my car back to the office so I can hitch a ride on the 'Copter? I need to get back to the city for a really important verdict in my friends trial."

"Sure Cathy," Tom said.

On the way back to the office Cathy thought about the morning, she knew this had to be the biggest story of the year. It would be all over the national and world news, but her enthusiasm was tempered by the ghoulish details. She knew there would be endless investigation involved to dig out all the facts in this story. She also knew that since she had been the one to break the story, she had a good chance of staying in charge of it.

Chapter Twenty Four:

James left the hotel early the next morning so he could get to the courthouse before the demonstrators.

He might as well have slept a few more hours. The demonstrators were already out in force. This morning the placards were more damning. "Dr. Hartley, Frankenstein Monster", "Dr. "Ghoul" Barnett" and "Dr. God" were just a few. He made his way through the crowd and into the relative quiet of the building. He thought about Cathy's' phone call and he hoped Chase would arrive before he heard of the F.B.I. raid so James could be the one to tell him about it. The minutes ticked off, but no Chase. It was still early, but he thought he should be there by now. Finally he arrived, "Sorry I'm late James it has been a hectic morning."

"Have you heard the news from Kingman?" James asked. Chase was surprised by the question. "Yes I have, but how did you hear about it?"

"Cathy called me this morning; she's covering it for her paper." James said. "Is this going to cause trouble for you?"

"I don't think so; NSCT was cloning for years before I joined them. My research improved their success rate from 13% to over 97%, but I have not been involved in the harvesting process, in fact, I've never even visited Kingman, I do all my research at Half Moon Bay. My non-destructive electron transfer system has great promise for the future of cloning, James."

James looked around to the gallery, he saw Brent's' brother, Henry, but Ann was not with him. He knew Cathy could not be there, but he looked for her anyway.

"All rise; Hear Ye, Hear Ye, the Superior Court of the City of San Francisco is now in session. The Honorable Judge Ernst Wilson presiding," the bailiff announced as Judge Wilson entered and took his seat at the bench. "Please be seated and come to order."

"The prosecution may continue cross examination," the Judge said. "Will Dr. Chase Hartley please take the stand."

Chase was sworn in. "Dr. Hartley" the D.A. began with his questions,"Yesterday you testified that you were Dr. Chase Hartley and Dr. Brent Alswerp, do I have that correct?"

"Yes"

"Can you explain to those of us not possessing great intellect, how this could be possible?"

"Dr. James Barnett removed the frontal parietal lobe in my brain and transplanted it in the brain of Chase Hartley. I have been living incognito in the physical body of Dr. Hartley."

“Are you aware Dr. Hartley that we have had expert testimony that the type of operation you describe would be utterly impossible to perform successfully?”

“Because something has never been done does not preclude its future success.”

“What is your date of birth Dr. Hartley?”

“January 10th, 1952.”

“That would make you 58 years old, Dr. Hartley; you look to be half that age.”

“Precisely.”

“So you still claim to be Dr. Brent Alswerp living in Dr. Chase Hartley’s body?”

“Yes”

“Can you explain to us why you make this claim?

“When I get up in the morning, I know who I am. When I go to bed at night, I know who I am. Who I am is the same as who I was for 58 years.”

“I have here a research paper by Dr. Alswerp from his early work. There is a graph on page 12. Would you explain the meaning of this data, Dr. Hartley?”

“The graph depicts the data I obtained by experiments with college students to determine the location of the “sense of self" but this is not the version that appeared in the final report because we found an error when we ran a regression analysis of the data. The error was corrected in the final version."

"I see." The D.A. had hoped for a less definitive answer. This wasn't going well, he thought.

"Are you married Dr. Hartley?" He asked.

"I was married."

"But are you married now?"

"No"

"And why is that?"

"I was declared dead on March 14, 2008"

"And were the proceeds from your life insurance policy paid to your wife?"

"I don't know."

"I can answer that for you, Dr. Hartley, Mrs. Ann Alswerp received a $ 500,000.00 payment from American National Insurance Company because you were declared dead on March 14th. Are you claiming that payment was made in error? Do you believe that money should be returned?"

"No"

"And why is that?"

"Because, within the parameters of our society; I was declared dead on March 14th."

"No further questions, Your Honor."

"Does the defense wish to question the witness?" Judge Wilson asked.

"Yes, Your Honor." Sherman began, "Dr. Hartley, you came here at great personal sacrifice to testify at this trial, can you tell the court why you did that?"

"Dr. Barnett agreed to help me carry on my life and my work by performing an extremely delicate and challenging operation which was unheard of in the medical community. He did it because he had faith in the research I presented to him and his trust in my integrity. I could not remain silent while I watched him stand trial for a crime he didn't commit."

"Objection, hearsay," the D.A. said.

"Objection sustained, clerk will strike the response from the record," Judge Wilson said.

"In testimony from Dr. Nerneau and Dr. Barnett they stated that you pleaded with them to perform the transplant operation, is that true?" Sherman asked.

"I'm afraid I can't answer that."

"Why is that Dr. Alswerp?" "Objection, the witness has not been proven to be Dr. Alswerp." "Objection sustained."

"Why is it you can't answer doctor?"

"I have memory loss for a period of three months prior to the operation."

"If in fact you are Dr. Alswerp, can you tell me where you grew up as a child?" Sherman asked

"324 Ashland Avenue, Detroit, Michigan."

"And the name of the school you attended for first grade?"

"It was Thirkle, I remember it well because at that age everyone would correct me and say 'you mean Circle' to which I would reply no, it is Thirkle."

"Let the record show the answers given are correct for Dr. Alswerp's childhood. Thank you Dr. Hartley, no further questions, Your Honor."

"Court will take a short recess. When we resume we will continue the final arguments." Judge Wilson rapped his gavel.

A short time later, the Bailiff returned with his familiar cry.

"All rise; Hear Ye, Hear Ye, the Superior Court of the City of San Francisco is now in session. The Honorable Judge Ernst Wilson presiding," the bailiff announced as Judge Wilson entered and took his seat at the bench. “Please be seated and come to order.”

“The prosecutor may continue his closing argument.”

“Thank you Your Honor. Ladies and gentlemen of the jury, you have witnessed testimony in this case that is not just unique but bordering on the bizarre. Never before, in the annals of criminal trials, has a jury been asked to accept testimony from a witness who claims to be the reincarnated soul of a dead man. I don’t think I need to point out to you that you should question the credibility of this witness. The defense would have you believe that Dr. James Barnett, who, by his own admission, cut open the skull of Dr. Brent Alswerp, removed his brain and left the ‘carcass’ dead on the operating table, did not actually commit murder. You can reach only one conclusion, ladies and gentlemen; Dr. James Barnett is guilty of second degree murder.”

The D.A. Returned to his table confident that the jury would bring back a guilty verdict.

“The defense may resume their closing argument,” Judge Wilson said.

“Thank you, Your Honor. Ladies and gentlemen of the jury, you have witnessed testimony that no jury has ever had the opportunity to hear. This trial will be remembered and referenced long after every one of us is gone. History has been made here. The world has to accept a new meaning of “life after death.” After all, what is “death?” Is it, as the dictionary says, “total and permanent cessation of all the vital functions of an organism?” If this is our definition, then how can we believe that the permanent cessation of all vital functions of Dr. Brent Alswerp’s brain occurred on that operating table when we have unquestionable proof that his brain is alive and well in the body of Dr. Chase Hartley?” You watched as the prosecutor tried to discredit our witness with questions only Dr. Alswerp could possibly answer. You watched as the witness recalled memories of his brother that obviously only he could have known. Chase Hartley, a former baseball player, after receiving the brain transplant from Dr. Alswerp, has astounded professors and colleagues alike with his brilliance. Since his graduation from Med School with top honors, Dr. Chase Hartley has been building upon the pioneering neurological research of Dr. Alswerp. Your decision here today, ladies and gentlemen, will be remembered and debated for years to come. Is life defined by the shell we occupy, or is it defined by “who we are” inside that shell. Dr. Alswerp is alive in the shell of Dr. Hartley.”

“Does a hermit crab believe he is a snail because he inhabits a snails shell? No, the shell is not important ladies and gentlemen.”

Sherman looked the jurors straight in the eyes, “What makes us unique? Can you imagine being me and not you? Of course not. We can’t imagine being someone else because we are who we are. No matter where we are or what we are doing we are always the person we know as ourselves. When we look in the mirror we don't see who we are, we see what we are. We are an accumulation of goals achieved, dreams dashed, success and failure, choices made with our conscience as our guide and our connection to a higher power.

It was the genius of Dr. Alswerp and the expertise of Dr. Barnett that enabled him to pluck the plum of "who we are" from Dr. Alswerp's brain and implant it into the brain of Chase Hartley.

Dr. Barnett has testified that he felt the 'hand of God' assisting him during the operation. Perhaps our good Lord has provided us with a means of extending the lives of those who can contribute so much to the welfare of mankind.

This trial has provided irrefutable evidence of mans' ingenuity in his quest for immortality, one lifetime at a time."

Sherman returned to the table for the defense, patting James on the shoulder as he sat down.

Judge Wilson read his instructions to the jury. When he finished with the 'boiler-plate', he added "When I tell you that a party must prove something, they must persuade you by the evidence presented in court, that what they are trying to prove is more likely to be true than not true. You may retire for your deliberations."

As the jury filed out, James sat back and contemplated his fate. Within the next few hours, he would learn whether he was a free man or if he would spend the rest of his life in prison. He decided not to dwell on the latter until the verdict was in. "James," Sherman said, "It may be a while before they come up with a verdict, do you want to get something to eat?"

"No thanks, you go ahead, I want to chat with my friend," James said as he made his way over to Chase. He didn't want to go outside the courtroom and have to contend with the demonstrators.

"It's all over now, except for the waiting," Chase said as James approached.

"The waiting and the shouting," James said, referring to the demonstrators. "I saw the Kingman raid on the news this morning, Chase; it looks like things could get nasty. If I can help you out in any way, please be sure to call on me, assuming of course that I am not locked up."

"Thanks James, but I really don't expect any personal problems with the issue, but the company will have some explaining to do."Chase said as Henry joined them and said, "James, I want to apologize to you, I had no idea what was going on and this jerk brother of mine, looking at Chase as he said it, didn't help things by keeping everything so secret. You know Brent, I know you're in there, but when I look at you, all I see is Chase Hartley." "Sorry, Henry, I know it is confusing." Chase said.

Just then Cathy came rushing up to them. "James, how are you, I left Kingman the minute I could get away. The jury's still out, right? I wanted to be here when they brought in the verdict."

"So, little lady, you have stirred up a hornets' nest in Kingman." Chase said to Cathy.

"I'm sorry Chase, but I hope you didn't know about everything that was going on down there," she said.

"No Cathy, I've never been down there," Chase said, "but they have been operating the last few years with my automated system of fertilization."

Cathy broke in, "Well, as you know, human cloning in Arizona is legal, but holding the clones in detention is certainly not legal, nor is disposing of failed attempts."

"What do you mean "disposing?" Chase said.

"You didn't know about that? What do you think happened to all the clones that were born with deformities, or developed sicknesses, or aged prematurely? Cathy looked at Chase for his reaction. He was obviously uncomfortable.

"They were supposed to be cared for in the hospital on the site," Chase answered.

"I'm afraid that just didn't happen" Cathy said.

A bailiff circulated among them in the courtroom. "The jury is returning," he said.

Cathy and Chase sat in the front of the gallery right behind James as the jurors filed in. Sherman and the D.A. staff took their places.

"All rise; Hear Ye, Hear Ye, the Superior Court of the City of San Francisco is now in session. The Honorable Judge Ernst Wilson presiding," the bailiff announced as Judge Wilson entered and took his seat at the bench.

"Please be seated and come to order. Has the jury reached a verdict?"

"We have, Your Honor," the jury foreman handed a paper to the bailiff who took it over to the judge. Judge Wilson looked at it and handed it to the clerk. Cathy thought she saw a faint smile cross his face as he looked in their direction. "The defendant will please stand. The clerk will read the verdict."

"In the case of the State of California versus Dr. James Barnett, violation of California Penal Code 401, the jury finds the defendant not guilty."

Cathy and Chase jumped up, hugging each other as James turned around and joined in a three way hug with the railing separating them. "Thank you Lord," James said. "Amen," said Cathy.

Chapter Twenty Five:

They stepped out of the courthouse into a maelstrom. The demonstrators hounded them. "Witch Doctor" and "Devil Doctor" placards were shoved in James' face. Microphones and TV cameras were thrust at them. "What's it like to be God?" "Who's next, Dr. Barnett?" "Do you think what you did was ethical?" They were jostled as they forced their way toward their car.

Chase was being attacked in equal fashion. "How many clones have you made?" "What are you going to do with the clones?" "Will the clones get new brains, Dr. Hartley?" "What happens to the defective clones?" Cathy recognized some of the media were her people. It seemed really strange to be on the other side of the cameras.

Chase hollered over the tumult, "I'll call you James," as he disappeared into the crowd.

James took Cathy to his car and they climbed in to escape the demonstrators. "We'll come back later for your car, Cathy," James said as they pulled away from the curb slowly so as not to injure any of the demonstrators. "How about we have a drink at the hotel lounge?" James said.

"Perfect," Cathy answered. The Kingman story was on every TV in the bar. "We have breaking news from San Francisco," the anchor was saying, "The murder trial of Dr. James Barnett came to a dramatic end today with an ironic twist.

Testimony from Dr. Chase Hartley, the mystery recipient of Dr. Brent Alswerp's brain convinced the jury that he was indeed Dr. Alswerp. The jury acquitted Dr. Barnett of the charges against him."

"The irony here is that Dr. Hartley is connected to our other top story, the cloning farm uncovered by San Jose Times investigative reporter Cathy Nichols."

"As we have been reporting with news breaks throughout the day, the FBI raided a human cloning farm operated by NSCT in Kingman, Arizona. Surrogate mothers were employed to carry the fetuses to birth. The clones were housed and schooled within the compound, but it is the disposition of the defective clones that has the nation in an uproar."

"Later in our program we will have video of an explosion at the medical facility in the compound that killed several clones and the medical director. Criminal charges are expected to be filed against several employees of NSCT that the FBI has in custody."

"Let's sit where we don't have to hear the TV," Cathy said. They settled in to a comfortable booth in the corner and ordered Margaritas.

"It's a Margarita night," James said.

"I agree," Cathy nodded.

"Well girl, how do you feel about receiving credit for the Kingman thing on national news?" James said.

"You know, it's something I have dreamed of for years, and it is very satisfying, but right now my mind is much more concerned with us. When are you returning to Chicago?" Cathy asked.

"Wow, talk about getting to the heart of the matter," James said.

"I have never been one to skirt an issue," She said.

"The answer to your question is; I don't know, I should get back to my practice, but I don't want to leave you. What would you say to the idea of coming back to Chicago with me?"

"Is that a proposal or a proposition," Cathy asked jokingly, because she knew it was neither.

"Seriously Cathy, I didn't think it was possible to fall in love with someone in such a short time, but I think we need more time together before we make a lifetime commitment. That's why I made my suggestion, but how do you feel Cathy?"

"James, I love you to death, you know I do, but I think you are right, we really haven't known each other long enough to make that kind of decision, so that kind of leaves us in long distance limbo, doesn't it?"

"I couldn't leave right now with this story breaking. It's going to be a while before things quiet down." Frustrated by the strain she knew the separation would put on their relationship, Cathy was not optimistic about their future.

"I'm frightened, James, what is going to happen to us?"

The adrenaline that had kept Cathy going for the past 24 hours was ebbing and she was exhausted. Cathy and James fell asleep that night wrapped in the arms of the other, trying to hold on tight to the love they shared. Could their love withstand the imminent separation facing them? The thought was weighing heavily upon them.

When Cathy awoke she heard the sound of James in the shower. "Should I go in and try for an encore of yesterday morning?" she wondered. "Or should I just lie here and pretend to be asleep until he comes out?" This morning they were going separate ways and she didn't know how to handle it.

"Hey Cathy, need a back scrub?" James shouted from the shower.

"What the hell," she said to herself, "I'll figure it out later."

"Coming James," she yelled out.

Cathy joined him in the shower and let the warm soapy water wash over her as James hands caressed her body. She enjoyed these few moments of bliss before the sorrow of their parting overtook her once again.

They dried off from their shower and dressed for the drive to the airport. They went through the motions of packing and loading James luggage into the car with heavy hearts.

They were in a solemn mood as Cathy drove James to the airport and stopped in front of the terminal. They sat together trying to find the words to ease their parting. "What can I say that I haven't said already?" Cathy thought. "I'll write, I'll miss you, I love you, be good." Nothing could be said that would ease the pain of what they were feeling at that moment.

James looked at Cathy, the sadness in his eyes made her reach over to him. He held onto her hand and mouthed the words, "I love you," and then he opened the door and reached into the back for his luggage. He took one last look at Cathy as he closed the door and walked into the terminal.

Walking down the boarding ramp, James could hardly put one foot in front of the other. When he reached his seat he looked back at the terminal. "I still have time to grab my bag and get off the plane," he thought. He had never been so conflicted. He wanted to stay with Cathy, but he had to get back to his practice. He had been away too long already and he couldn't jeopardize what he had worked so hard to build. As the plane pushed back from the gate, he felt the finality of their parting. Is this the last time I see her, he wondered.

Cathy threw herself into her work. Kingman was turning out to be the journalistic powerhouse that she had expected and she was immersed in a whirlwind of activity surrounding it from morning 'til night. It was only at night when lying in bed that she thought about James and what he was doing and what they may be doing if he was with her.

"Cathy!" Peters' voice could be heard throughout the newsroom, as usual.

"Yes Peter," she said as she went into his office.

"Tell me Cathy, why is it after I put my heart and soul into training someone, and they become half-way competent the mega station vultures try to lure them away?" Peter was feigning anger, but she could tell he was pleased.

"What is it Peter?" Cathy asked, hopeful that he was talking about her.

"WCBC, in New York, they seem to think you would make a great investigative reporter and co-anchor of their six o'clock news."

She ran around Peter's desk and hugged him around the neck. "You're not kidding, are you Peter," she asked, thinking this was too good to be true.

"No Cathy, it's real, they want you up there tomorrow afternoon for interviews," Peter said.

"I can't do that, I already have appointments for tomorrow," she said.

"You can do it," Peter replied.

Cathy spent her time on the plane to New York wondering if she would get the job, what it would cost for an apartment, what would happen to her Kingman story and what, if any, effect this would have on her relationship with James. They had kept in close touch by phone since he went back to Chicago and when she told him about WCBC he seemed uneasy about her living in New York. She decided to wait until after the interview to call him again. At least Chicago was closer to New York than it was to San Jose.

The cab dropped her off in front of WCBC headquarters in Manhattan. Impressive, to say the least Cathy thought as she looked up at the thirty story building with WCBC engraved in the marble over the entrance. She approached the receptionist on the 28th floor "My name is Cathy Nichols I'm here to see the program director Mr. Whitney," she said.

"Oh yes, Ms. Nichols, Mr. Whitney has been waiting for you," she replied.

"Cathy," a strong greeting emanated from the imposing man approaching her. "John Whitney, how are you Cathy?"

"I'm fine, I think," she replied.

"Come in my office where we can talk for a few minutes before we meet with Mr. Bruening, our V.P. of Production." He continued, "Peter speaks very highly of your work and of course we have seen what you have done with the Kingman story." Cathy felt comfortable with this man and when he introduced her to Mr. Bruening she was impressed with his 'hands on' approach to his job and his grasp of the TV news industry. She could work with these people, she thought, and when they offered her the position of co-anchor and investigative reporter she accepted with only a slight feeling of fear. "This is the Big Apple," she thought and she hoped she would fit in.

Her brain was swimming on the plane ride back to California. She thought about the line in the song, "If you can make it here you can make it anywhere." She got the job but now she had to prove herself once again to a new organization, find an apartment, move her things and close out her appointments at the station. She would earn more than twice as much in New York, but she knew her living expenses would be a lot higher. She hadn't been able to reach James, and she really wanted to tell him the news. She reached James on her drive home from the airport.

"That's great Cathy," he said, "When are you supposed to start?"

"In about two weeks, on the first of the month," she answered.

"Oh," was James' reply.

"You don't sound happy about this," Cathy said.

"I'm uneasy about you being alone in New York with no family or friends for support."

"I know, James, but I have been through this several times already, and I've always managed to make new friends."

"That's what bothers me," James thought.

James had settled into his routine, operating on Tuesdays and Thursdays and visiting patients the rest of the week. Weekends were for Gypsy. Whether he was racing or pleasure sailing, he enjoyed complete relaxation when he was on the boat.

James was in the office when he received the call from Ann. "Ann Alswerp is on the line," Janet announced.

"Hi Ann, how are you, I haven't seen you since the trial.

"That's what I called about Jimmy. After Chase testified I was so upset I could have killed him. You probably saw that I slapped his face."

"Yes, I saw that," James said.

"I felt he had tricked me into a relationship, but when I learned how many unknown variables were involved in the operation and what could have been a disastrous outcome for everyone, I can understand why there was the need for secrecy. I'm also not sure I could have handled the media frenzy. Anyway, I tried to call him, but the company said he was on a leave of absence. Do you have a number for him?" Ann sounded quite upset.

"No, Ann, I don't have a number for him, but he called me the day before yesterday and said he was provisioning Adagio for an extended cruise. He was fed up with the harassment from the media. They wouldn't leave him alone Ann, even though he wasn't responsible, they hounded him over the 'human cloning factory'. It sounded like he was going to be sailing soon, possibly in the morning." James hoped the information would be helpful. Ann and Chase were both good friends and he would like to help them get together.

"Thanks, Jimmy, you have been a big help," she said, and added, "How have you been managing with the media?"

"It has been pure Hell Ann, for a while they were practically following me into the bathroom but it is slackening off now. My main problem now is with all the people who are hounding me to be cloned, so I know what Chase was going through. But hey Ann, It was really nice hearing from you." James said, and wondered what the future might hold for Ann and Chase.

Cathy was excited about her new job. She had always wanted an anchor job, and she was not disappointed. She liked being 'on camera' although it didn't leave as much time for her to do the investigative reporting that she enjoyed. She did meet some new friends, although none that James should have to worry about. They still talked on the phone almost every night, but she missed the intimacy of direct contact. Days turned to weeks and weeks turned to months and she and James had not been able to arrange a weekend together. Cathy was hosting a party for some of her co-workers from the station one night when James called. Cathy was carrying a tray of Hors D'oeuvres when the phone rang and she asked Martin to answer it for her. "Who answered the phone?" James immediately wanted to know.

"Martin Pierce, he's my co-anchor," Cathy answered.

"Oh, hey Cathy I know you're busy so give me a call later, OK?" James said as he hung up. A disquieting feeling was overcoming him. He didn't want to lose Cathy but he couldn't deny that they were slowly drifting apart. He didn't want to contemplate a future without Cathy in his life and decided to make a bold move. "Damn the torpedoes, full speed ahead," he thought.

The station asked her to take a camera crew to do some interviews that staff had arranged with well known surgeons at the International Neurological Symposium. She finished her first interview and was moving on to the next as she glanced at the chart for the name, Dr. James Barnett. She looked at the chart again, her knees about to buckle, was it really him?

"Hi Cathy," came the familiar voice from behind her. She turned around, her legs barely able to support her.

“James! It is you,” she managed to say.

As she faced him, he dropped to one knee and said, “Cathy, I love you, will you marry me?”

“Yes James, Yes, Yes, Yes.” She dropped onto her knees and kissed him hard, not thinking about the TV audience that was watching. She had never known the happiness she felt at that moment. They struggled to their feet, still clinging to each other.

“James, how did you do this?” she asked.

“Well, I received an invitation to speak at the symposium, and when I saw it was in New York, I contacted your boss and the rest is history,” he said a little smugly. “We have a lot of catching up to do, how much longer do you have to work?” James asked. Cathy looked at her camera man who gave her an approving nod and took the microphone from her hand.

“I guess I’m finished now,” she said. James took her arm and guided her through the crowd.

“Where would you like to have dinner?” he asked.

“How about your room?” she said. They rode the elevator to James’ room on the 12th floor. Cathy had trouble keeping her hands off him in the crowded elevator. As James put his card into the door lock, she was already unbuttoning her blouse. She had suppressed her longing for James for months and it was overwhelming her. He pushed the door open and held it for her to enter. She brushed past him and turned around and pulled him into her inside the door. Their hands were all over each other, searching for buttons and zippers as they shuffled toward the bed. James found the clasp on her bra and slid both his hands under her bra onto her bare breasts, kissing her on the neck as she was undoing his belt. She found the button at the top of his trousers and they dropped to his ankles. They were a tangled mess of humanity and clothing as they fell on the bed. "Time out," James said as he sat on the edge of the bed and took off his shoes and the rest of his clothing and pulled the covers down on the bed. By the time he finished, Cathy had already removed the rest of her clothes and bounced onto the sheets, putting her arms out to welcome him. Their bodies clamped together, arms entangled, her breasts rubbing against his chest, his hardness rubbing between her thighs.

"Cathy, I've dreamed of this for months," James said.

"Not only you," she whispered in his ear. Her insides were contracting in anticipation as she ran her hands caressingly over his body. He cupped her breasts in his hands as his mouth found her hardened nipples.

"Oh James, I've missed you so," she said, barely able to speak with the emotion overcoming her. His legs were in between hers and he moved up just enough so the head of his hardness was brushing against her. She maneuvered side to side, up and down. With each movement she could feel the head slipping almost imperceptibly further into her. She could have pushed against him to force it in, but she was enjoying the feeling of it going deeper little by little with each twist of her body. James was so considerate, she knew he was probably getting impatient, but he held back and let her control the pace of the insertion. He felt the warm juices swirling around his wand as it inched its way deeper toward its destiny. Cathy worked it into her until she had it all. James pulled back a bit and thrust. Oh my god, Cathy thought as it filled her up and the fireworks of her emotions began going off. Each thrust was better than the last and they were meeting thrust for thrust in perfect harmony. She wanted to go on forever, holding on to the rapture, never letting up, never letting go. She could tell James also wanted to hang on to the ecstasy of the moment, but the intoxication they were experiencing from their love was overwhelming them. Their breathing quickened, and as each one felt the other reaching their climax, it amplified the passion into a crescendo of shared emotion. The explosion could no longer be contained and it erupted in a screaming, clutching and convulsive conclusion to their union. James collapsed onto Cathy and rolled over on his back. After a few minutes of recovery, they turned on their sides, facing each other. James propped his head up on his arm, looking at Cathy with his soulful blue eyes and said "words cannot describe how fantastic that was." "I know," Cathy answered, "and just think, we have the rest of our lives to see if we can top it."

Epilogue:

Chase hadn't seen Ann since the trial when she slapped him on the face. He cursed himself for not being more forthright with her. Perhaps if he had told her early on who he really was, he might not have spoiled his chances. He could understand why she was so upset with him. He thought about the last time they were together. Ann had loved him with an abandon she had never displayed in the past. She had unleashed her emotions in a way he had never before experienced. She had made passionate love to a stranger in effect, in the presence of her late husband. She must feel shame and embarrassment from the incident. "Damn, why didn't I tell her who I was?" It's no wonder she was infuriated with him.

He thought about how everything had become really hectic after the last time they were together on the boat. James' trial had required all of his attention and the mayhem afterward made it impossible to conduct any meaningful research. He decided to take a break from his work until things quieted down. He had loaded enough provisions aboard "Adagio" for an extended cruise and made plans to sail down to the Baja Peninsula.

The weather forecast for the next few days looked ideal. He anticipated nice weather for his cruise as he headed for the Yacht Club. He always enjoyed the sereneness of the early morning just before sunrise. The orange glow mixing with the blue hues left over from the night sky lent an air of tranquility to the morning. He had a feeling of loneliness as he walked down the dock. He missed Ann.

When he reached the boat he noticed there were lights in the cabin and the companionway hatch was open. What the hell, he wondered. He smelled the aroma of freshly brewed coffee as he climbed aboard.

"Ann!" "What?" "How" he could only get one word out at a time.

"You didn't change the combination on the lock," she said, as if that was all the explanation that was required. He scrambled down the companionway and took her into his arms. "I've missed you so," he whispered into her ear. "I've missed you too," she whispered back. "Will you ever forgive me?" he asked. "Ever is a long time, ask me again in twenty years," Ann replied.

"I was going to leave on a cruise to Baja this morning," he said. Ann looked up into his eyes, "I know, I called James and he told me of your plans. Would you have room for a crew member? I have a lot of experience."

The sun was just coming over the horizon as "Adagio" cast off. "Take the wheel Ann." "I'll go forward and hoist the main. We'll be sailing a heading of WSW." Chase returned to the cockpit. "How's our heading Ann?" He noticed a twinkle in Ann's eyes as she smiled and said, "Right on course."

www.ingramcontent.com/pod-product-compliance
Lightning Source LLC
LaVergne TN
LVHW050622100826
845148LV00011B/1694